TAKEN BY THE ENFORCER

A DARK MAFIA SURPRISE BABY ROMANCE

TAKEN SERIES: LUCCHESE FAMILY
BOOK ONE

CHARMAINE LOUISE SHELTON

CONTENTS

Dear Reader,

Taken by the Enforcer is a dark mafia romance intended for 18+ mature readers only.

If you love possessive, dominant Alpha males, forced proximity, mafia danger, surprise baby tropes, and a heroine who finds her strength even when trapped, then welcome to *La Famiglia*.

If you need soft and safe? This isn't that book.

ABOUT TAKEN BY THE ENFORCER: A DARK MAFIA SURPRISE BABY ROMANCE

Want it. Take it. And I want the baby and her.

She may not like it, but. They. Are. Mine.

Donatello

Want it. Take it. That's the Lucchese way. That's my way.

I've watched Paolina Corsetti waste herself on a pathetic boy who never deserved her. The night she runs from her wedding, she runs straight into me.

Her tears taste like sin. Her body fits against mine like she was made for me.

And when she disappears and I find out she's pregnant with my child, I hunt her down.

She thinks she has a choice.

She doesn't. That curry *dolcezza* belongs to me.

Always has. Always will.

Paolina

Doesn't every bride cry on her wedding day?

I thought my tears would be from joy.

Instead, I'm sobbing into a cocktail after catching my fiancé screwing my former best friend.

That's when he appears.

Donatello Romano.

Tall, dark, and dangerously handsome—the Lucchese family's enforcer. My fiancé's boss. The man I should fear.

But when he lifts my fallen veil from the floor, one smoldering look unravels me. One reckless night leaves me staring at two pink lines.

Now I hide.

From the truth. From hum—the possessive man who hunts me down with a promise in his obsidian eyes: *I take what's mine.*

And he swears I'm his.

Me… and his baby growing inside me.

This isn't the marriage I expected.

But maybe it's the one my heart secretly wants.

Their spicy dark mafia secret baby romance is the stand-alone prequel to the Taken Series: The Lucchese Family. The interconnecting novels feature sexy as sin morally gray anti-heroes and the women who make their stony hearts beat. Get a glimpse of their dynamism in other books.

Anthem: "Belong To You" by Sabrina Claudio

https://youtu.be/6eug7Qv8iKY?si=
r0A0bwrbkVLy_PSc

Soundtrack
https://www.youtube.com/playlist?list=
PLXwYvn0e218CijTUk-zh40SsM0suh3ftS

Visit CharmaineLouiseBooks.com

CHAPTER 1

onatello

EACH TIME that fucker Aldo Buratti stands within 10 yards of me, I want to slice his goddamn throat. And tonight is no different.

"Donatello, we should kill the asshole. Get it over with already," the dick tap dancing on my last nerve pipes up.

This fucker right here.

As if he can decide for the Lucchese mafia family—the head of *La Cosa Nostra*. The most omnipotent crime family in the world based in Sicily with capos throughout Europe, Canada, and the United States. Now under Luca's control as Boss, the primary focus is arms dealers. Lucchese S.r.l.—known as an import/export company—provides the largest assortment of top-quality weaponry. Individuals and organizations seek us out for pistols to missiles, adding to the family's billions of dollars every hour. And they don't want to miss one euro. Or else.

"What made you think you could steal from the shipment and get away with it?"

I ignore Aldo and step closer to the fool dangling from the darkened warehouse ceiling. Naked, bruised, and bloody, his wrists swell in the chains wrapped around them. As he sways from the last punch to the gut, his toes draw trails in the filthy mixture of broken teeth, piss, and blood on the cement floor. A floor all too familiar with similar body fluids and guts.

My footsteps stop when the tips of my shoes reach the puddle. I cock my head to the side and study the fool's unrecognizable face. One eye swollen shut—I always leave one open so they can see what's coming next—nose smashed, lip busted. Not even his mother would know her son. And she'll never see him again.

I may not be a Lucchese. But for generations, the Romano family's role as top-level enforcers and assassins made us closer to the family than any of their capos. We take it personally when someone dares to go against the Luccheses—family or money.

"Donatello! Did you hear me?"

In an instant, I spin and backslap Aldo across the face. He grunts and stumbles sideways, eyes wide, clutching his reddened cheek. My obsidian eyes narrow on him, flashing with danger.

"Unless you want to hang beside this fool, shut. The. Fuck. Up."

He crumbles further beneath my withering stare, backing away in silence. Not until he returns in line with the other two soldiers do I refocus on the hanging man.

"Do not make me repeat myself."

His one good eye flicks behind me.

"I-I'm s-s-sorry, Donatello," he stutters around broken teeth. Blood mixed with saliva dribbles down his wobbling chin. He chokes and spits. "I-I never would have. Swear. Please…"

My fists pummel his stomach in rapid succession of blows. Blood expels from his mouth. Splatters stain my white dress shirt rolled up to my elbows. More blood from the open cuts in his torso covers my bare forearms. The fucker is lucky a bundle of fresh shirts remains on hand in the trunk of my Bugatti. My lip curls in disgust.

"You failed to answer my question. My patience ends."

I stride to the table. A variety of instruments line its surface. My eyes scan the pliers, brass knuckles, scalpels, pinchers, and more to extract answers from the unfortunate. This one cries for God when I lift the handsaw.

"You'll meet the devil soon enough. But first, I take the hand that dared to take from the Luccheses. Get him down."

Aldo and the soldiers rush forward.

"Wait! I'll tell you," the fucker cries, wild-eyed. At their approach, he thrashes, head swivels, and his chest heaves. "I'll tell you all!"

The strength only a dead man walking possesses has his arms flailing.

"No! It was—"

Bang!

A gunshot pierces the air, followed by two more close-range blasts.

Aldo kneels over the still body of the thief. Three holes gape open in his chest. Blank eyes stare unseeingly.

"The fuck you think you're doing?!" I thunder at Aldo. The two soldiers who jumped to their feet at the first gunshot glance between us warily. They know I do not tolerate disobedience. "I didn't give the order to kill him. You tried the last of my—"

"He reached for my gun. It was self-defense," Aldo says, staring at the dead man. He stands and faces me as he holsters his weapon. "My apologies, boss."

I assess his face and body language.

His eyes lower in respect. Beyond the change in demeanor, he remains unnerved. No sweat beads on his forehead, or eyes blink rapidly. Even his jaw remains relaxed. He stands before me, composed.

I flick my gaze to the other two. They shake their heads and raise their hands up, palms out. My gaze returns to Aldo. He brings his gaze to mine. My eyes narrow. He's unflinching.

I replay the scene in my head and recall nothing that

would contradict his self-defense answer. If he were lying, I'd kill him on the spot. But the code stays my hand.

"Clean this shit up," I snarl and pivot, stalking to the sink as I peel off the shirt. My muscles ripple with the movement. I toss the ruined shirt to the floor and twist the spigots angrily. The water splashes up from the basin to soak my shirt. A growl simmers in my chest.

As I wash blood from my hands and forearms, I watch them through the mirror's reflection. My gaze tracks Aldo's every move. He doesn't waver. But I can't stop the niggling in my gut. Then again, it could be because I can't stand the dick.

I dry off and ball up the shirt, careful not to get blood on me. Before I leave, I watch them clean up. They hose blood and gunk towards the drain at the center of the room while the fucker's body melts in a drum of hydro-fluoric acid. Satisfied with their progress, I stride for the door, only pausing to wipe the soles of my shoes on the mat they'll dispose of.

"*Buona notte*, D."

"See you, D."

I jerk my chin at the soldiers standing guard throughout the empty warehouse. It's one of many owned by the family. A burly soldier opens the door for me. His sharp gaze assesses the potential for threats in the night's shadowy surroundings of the warehouse. Only after he steps back with a nod, do I exit.

With a fresh shirt on, I slip into my suit jacket and slide behind the wheel of the supercar.

"Dammit!"

This is the second theft in four months, and I will find the backstabber.

The engine purrs to life. I shift gears and peel away from the warehouse, leaving Catania's port behind. Time to meet up with Marcello and Faustino at Club Petali.

I drive through the ancient streets of Sicily's second largest municipality until I pull up to elaborate black wrought-iron gates. A guard in a black suit steps from the security house at the entrance to the high-end men's club.

"Buonasera, Signore Romano," he says as he glances through my open window. I nod. Stepping back, he raises his left hand to signal for the guard in the security house to release the gates.

They swing outward, and I drive through. Cypress trees line the long driveway leading to a sprawling villa built millennia ago by a Roman prince for his mistress. The secluded estate and its provenance prove perfect for the luxury members-only club where the women willingly work to fulfill every fantasy. This location is one of many around the world owned by the Luccheses for the pleasure of the wealthy elite.

A valet—alerted of my arrival by the guard—waits to open my door as I stop at the foot of the villa's entry stairs. I jog up the stone steps to the front doors. A butler greets me as the glass and wrought-iron door opens.

The ceiling soars between twin staircases in the grand marble entrance. Prisms from the crystal chandeliers dazzle on the walls, drawing the eye to the themed salons. They flank the stairs with the gaming rooms beyond. The three upper floors serve as entertainment areas and as private suites, while the lower level and the cellar host darker fantasies. The seductive scent of vanilla and ylang-ylang wafts through the air. Sensual rhythmic music plays from a hidden surround-sound system, capturing the erotic ambiance of the villa. The club embodies the Lucchese's sense of old-world grandeur and luxury. Even a Mafia family prefers the best in life.

Waitstaff carry trays of prosecco and whiskey or of hors d'oeuvres in case the members prefer not to eat in the dining room or not to order drinks at the bars. I need a stronger drink. Food is the last thing on my mind. I shake my head as they approach.

Dozens of gorgeous, scantily clad women mill about on the arms or in the laps of men dressed in bespoke tuxedos. Not wanting their partners for the evening to notice but not wanting to miss their chance, the beauties wink surreptitiously at me as I pass. Mary I've bedded. Others want their chance. My reputation as a skilled lover runs rampant among them. But tonight, I'm here for business, not pleasure. I ignore their clandestine offers.

As I weave through the clusters, the members offer me their salutations. However, I don't linger. Marcello and Faustino await my arrival. Two soldiers stand outside the office. They nod as I stride past them to the door.

My older brother—by a year to my twenty-six—glances up from his mobile where he sits on the leather sofa. Eyes like mine scan my face for answers to the questions Marcello will have for me.

The youngest of the four Lucchese sons, he rose from an assassin to a family capo. Best friends since we were little, he brought Faustino and me on as his second and his third. He too studies my face.

"Nothing," I answer their silent query as I stride to the wet bar and pour two fingers of whiskey into a tumbler. I throw it back. The amber liquid burns down my throat but does little to dull my anger. It's not enough to displace the shitshow interrogation. I refill the glass, then face them. "I was about to relieve him of his hand when Aldo shot him dead. In self-defense."

"How the hell did that happen?"

I shrug an eyebrow, still pissed.

"Aldo says the fucker reached for his gun as he and two soldiers loosened him from the chains. It happened fast, and neither of the other two nor I can dispute it."

Faustino sucks his teeth and sighs. Marcello leans back in his leather chair and rubs the nape of his neck.

"Luca wants answers," he states flatly. His mink brown eyes bore into me with an unspoken warning. The stare cuts deeper than any scalpel I use during my interrogations. Message received loud and clear.

I finish the whiskey in one gulp, slamming the tumbler on the bar's smooth mahogany surface. I nod.

"He will have them."

CHAPTER 2

aolina

"Oh, *mia cara*, how beautiful you are! Aldo will be so pleased. What a perfect match your father made for you! Smile. You should be excited on your wedding day, Paolina."

Mamma's voice floats over the rustle of tulle as she fluffs the skirt yet again. She glances toward my open bedroom door, then turns back and whispers, "Unlike mine. Your father has always been a stern man. Thank God for his choice for you." Her moss-green eyes—so like mine—soften as she makes the sign of the cross. Lips touch pinched fingers; a prayer seals behind them.

I follow her lead out of habit more than such devoted faith.

On paper, this arranged marriage looks faultless. Aldo Buratti is handsome, connected, and eager to climb. That's what *Papà* values—ambition that serves the Family. Me? I'm the dutiful daughter of a made-man, so I nod when I'm told and smile when I should.

The smile doesn't reach my chest today. Something there feels tight and splintered.

Two months ago, Aldo proposed at our dining room table over cannoli Mamma made special. Powdered sugar dusted his lips, and I remember thinking the sweetness didn't belong to him. My yes fell out anyway because Papà's gaze pinned me to my chair. Ever since, he's controlled every detail, even the dress—a froth of tulle with puffed sleeves and a high neckline that turns me into a porcelain doll someone forgot to love. Even my stockings and shoes shout child-bride more than woman, despite my being twenty.

Mamma fastens the last pearl button at my nape. "Perfect," she sighs, stepping back to admire the version of me she helped create. "Cara will bring your bouquet when we arrive."

Cara. My best friend since primary school. My maid of honor. The girl who knows the truest version of me— curvy, stubborn, soft in secret places, eyes full of stories I never quite say aloud. She'll stand beside me and whisper jokes when my hands shake. The thought warms me, if only for a moment.

Papà's tread sounds in the hall. The air changes the way rooms do when iron enters. He fills the doorway in his tailored suit, graying hair slicked back, jaw set like a verdict. *"È l'ora,"* he says. It's time. The words leave no room for anything but obedience.

I lower my gaze and gather my skirts. *"Sì, Papà."*

The chauffeured car waits at the base of our steps, polished to a mirror so crisp I could touch the reflection of this girl in white and ask her to run. Instead, I slide inside, veil spilling over my lap like a small, captured cloud. Catania passes in soft gray stone and sun-faded walls, saints tucked into niches, balconies sagging with geraniums. People step aside when we sweep through. Everyone knows the Corsetti name; everyone smiles with the appropriate amount of teeth.

Santa Maria del Carmelo rises white and solemn from its square, bells tolling in measured beats that thud against my ribs. The scent of beeswax and citrus blossoms greets us at the doors. A few of Papà's men bracket the entrance in black suits, expressions smooth as slate. I step between them, Mamma on my arm, nods and murmurs pressing in from both sides as the church swallows us.

The bridal room is small and cool, with a crucifix centered on the wall as if to supervise. Mamma adjusts my veil again because she needs to do something. "Cara will be right back, *tesoro.* She went to find the florist about the ribbon on your bouquet."

I nod. No words, or too many will pour out.

The murmured conversation of guests drifts through the door—clinks, footsteps, the velvet hush of ritual moving into position. I stare at my reflection. Raven-dark hair coils in a heavy twist at my crown, anchored with pins that bite. The heart-shaped face looking back shows pink cheeks and perfectly painted lips. I look like a bride in a magazine. I feel like a girl beneath a wave.

"Just a minute to pray," I say, and Mamma's eyes mist. She squeezes my hands, grateful that piety still clings to me like lace.

"Of course." She kisses my cheek. "I'll check that the musicians are ready. Don't be long."

The hall beyond is hushed, carpet muffling my steps as I slip away. The confessional sits at the side of the nave, carved wood dark with age, a small red candle winking its one-eyed blessing. Kneel, speak, be absolved—simple steps I've known since childhood. Today I want quiet more than permission.

My fingers brush the curtain on the penitent's side, but something halts me. A low sound leaks from within. Not murmured prayer. A breath. A sigh. Another sound follows—soft at first, then unmistakable, paced and damp with need.

Blood drains to my feet.

Carefully, I ease my veil back and test the priest's door instead. It yields under my hand. The tiny chamber opens around me with its faint incense ghost and the rustle of fabric. I don't mean to look. I don't mean to see anything but shadow.

The shadows are full of bodies.

Aldo's broad back fills the narrow space, tuxedo

jacket rucked to his hips, trousers shoved low. His hands bracket bare thighs wrapped in cream ribbon garters I recognize because we picked them together. Cara's head tips back, a waterfall of chestnut hair catching on the wood as she bites her lip around a swallowed moan. One of her shoes dangles from a toe, bouncing in a rhythm that matches his thrusts.

I don't make a sound, not even a gasp. That's the most shocking part—this silence that grips my throat like a hand. Aldo's profile flashes when he turns to mutter something filthy, and I memorize the curve of his grin because I will need it later when I don't believe any of this was real.

Heat rises in my face. Not the heat that makes me dizzy when a man looks at my lush body like I'm a feast. This is scalding, chemical, a burn that strips skin bare.

Cara's fingers slide down her own belly, over the lace of her panties wedged embarrassingly high. She laughs—breathy, triumphant. "Hurry. We have to go back."

"After," Aldo pants, voice low and rough. "After I remind you who you belong to."

Belong. The word hits like a slap. For months I've been trying to sew that word onto myself like a patch—belong to Papà's plans, belong to Aldo's ambition, belong to a future that doesn't care if I fit. My stomach lurches.

I reverse one slow step, then another, palms slick against the doorframe. The old wood complains with a whisper. Aldo stiffens. Cara's eyes open, head turning toward the sound.

The door eases shut before her gaze finds mine.

For a second I lean into the wood, cheek pressed to splinters as if the confessional can confess for me. Knees want to give. Breath rasps in and out, too loud in this sanctuary where God watches everything and does nothing.

Get out. Now.

Veil gathered, skirts lifted just enough to keep from tripping, I slip along the side aisle toward the sacristy. A statue of the Madonna watches with a sorrow I finally understand. The world tilts. My feet keep moving because movement is the only thing that makes sense.

The sacristy door opens onto a surprised altar boy balancing a silver tray of cruets. He startles. I force my mouth to work. "Bathroom?" The single word scrapes my throat raw.

He points down a small corridor. "Second door, signorina."

I nod and keep going, but I don't stop at the bathroom. A side exit stands ajar, light knifing in, the smell of diesel and oranges riding the breeze. Beyond it, the courtyard bakes in the Sicilian sun. Doves hop along the wall. A cat sleeps in a rectangle of shade, tail twitching like a metronome.

The first sob tears loose then, loud in the quiet. I slap a hand over my mouth and taste salt and lipstick. Another sob shakes free. Then the flood comes, and my eyes burn, and I'm suddenly so tired of being an obedient daughter, a perfect fiancée, a proper anything.

Cara's laugh echoes in my head. Aldo's grunt follows, ugly and smug. The sound turns me hollow.

There's a bench under a lemon tree, and I sink onto it because my legs refuse to hold me. Perfumed shade drapes over my shoulders. A bee fusses with a blossom. Life goes on even when yours splits down the middle.

A shadow falls across the stones. "Signorina?" The sacristan—round, white-haired, kind—stands in the doorway, concern knitting his brows. "Are you unwell? Should I fetch your mother?"

A lie jumps to my tongue. A truth claws from underneath.

"I—" The word shreds. I swallow hard, smooth the front of the dress with shaking palms. "I needed air. *Per favore*, no one yet. Just a minute."

He studies my face, sees more than I want, and nods with grave delicacy. "*Un minuto*," he agrees, and slips away, closing the door enough to make me feel hidden.

Birdsong fills the courtyard. I focus on the lemon's skin, pores catching light, that faint oily gleam of zest. One breath. Then another. The sharp scent clears a little space in my head where thoughts can line up.

What do I do?

Aldo will be at the altar pretending he didn't just— My throat closes around the verb. Cara will smooth her hair and paint on the same glossy loyalty she swore to me last night. Papà will make deals with his eyes while the priest talks about vows. Mamma will cry for a future that no longer exists.

The word future doesn't sit right; it teeters and collapses. Everything inside me scrambles to fill the hole.

Running isn't brave. Running is survival.

I stand. Lemon petals stick to my veil; I pluck them free and watch them drift down like tiny white confetti. My hand finds the hidden zipper sewn into the side of the skirt for quick changes—something the seamstress suggested when Papà insisted on the layers. I tug, tug again, then breathe easier when the bodice slackens and air returns to my lungs.

A knock taps on the sacristy door. "Paolina?" Mamma's voice, careful and bright, the way she speaks to stray kittens. "*Tesoro*, the procession is forming."

My heart slams once. Twice. "Coming," I call, and marvel that the word comes steady. My legs carry me back through the small corridor, veil gathered close as armor. The bathroom door gapes. I duck inside and lock it.

In the mirror, a stranger stares back—cheeks blotched, eyes rimmed, lips trembling. I press cold water against my face with cupped hands, flinching at the shock, then pat dry with a towel too white for what I want to do with it. My palm trembles over the tiny pearl buttons. No time. No courage for that fight with a row of mother-of-pearl.

From the small window above the sink, I see the lane that runs along the church toward the piazza. A bar anchors the corner—La Sirena—blue awning fluttering, men clustered at high tables with espresso cups and little glasses of grappa. Life. Noise. An option that isn't this.

Another knock. Papà this time, voice like a blade wrapped in velvet. *"Figlia. Adesso."*

A lifetime fits into a heartbeat.

I unlock the door and step out. "One more moment," I say, brushing past him before his hand can close on my arm. "Just to collect myself."

He doesn't follow, because men like my father don't chase. They command. They expect the world to bend. Today, the world bends around me. Just this once.

The side exit yawns again, and I slip through like a shadow. The sun strikes, blinding bright. Every bead on my veil catches fire. Steps carry me across the courtyard, along the lane, toward the awning and the burst of voices. A delivery scooter zips past, horn peeping. No one notices the bride with tears drying on her cheeks because Sicily has seen stranger things than a girl deciding she won't let anyone sacrifice her on an altar of convenience.

La Sirena hums with afternoon talk and the clink of glass. I hover at the threshold, breath hitching, pulse a drum solo. Heads turn. Conversations pause. The bartender glances up—olive skin, sleeve tattoos, smile quick and easy. He doesn't stare. He just nods like brides wander in every day.

"Signorina?"

"Grappa," I say, surprising myself, then amend, "No. Something sweet."

"Amara e dolce." Bitter and sweet. He understands. A glass appears, amber liquid catching sunlight.

"On the house," he adds, eyes kind. *"Auguri."*

Congratulations. The word nearly undoes me.

My laugh is jagged. If only he knew. I lift the glass and drink anyway.

Warmth unfurls under my ribs. The sugar tells my brain I'm not dying. The bitter whispers the truth—I am changing.

"Cara!" a familiar voice trills from the corner near the window. My head whips before I can stop it. For one terrified instant I think she's followed me, but it's only a woman greeting her friend with the same name. My lungs restart.

I finish the drink. The room steadies. The mirror behind the bar reflects the door and the street beyond. If anyone comes looking, I'll see them before they see me. For the first time today, I feel... not safe exactly, but possible. Like a different ending just opened and beckoned me through.

The bells begin again, tolling for a bride who won't walk that aisle.

Aldo will notice, and Papà will seethe, and Mamma will cry, and Cara will pretend, but none of that belongs to me anymore. Not after what I saw in the priest's dark box where sins are supposed to be cleaned, not committed.

I shake my head to clear the thoughts. The veil is heavy in my lap, damp with tears and citrus-scented air just as my dress—the monstrosity of white tulle Papà chose—billows around the stool like some kind of cage. A bride drinking alone? What a spectacle.

The door opens, sending a shaft of sunlight across the floor. I don't look up right away, too busy choking back the next sob. But I hear it—the solid thud of boots, the hush that follows when someone powerful walks into a room.

Then I sense him before I see him.

CHAPTER 3

 aolina

BUT IT'S NOT ALDO.

Donatello Romano.

The name alone should make my blood run cold. Enforcer for the Lucchese family. Aldo's boss. Papà's associate. Dangerous doesn't even begin to describe the man who makes hardened criminals piss themselves with a single stare.

One breath and I'm back, a year ago.

The chandelier at Teatro Massimo Bellini scatters light like diamonds across silk and shoulders, every facet catching in the air scented with orange blossom and polished wood. A string quartet plays something lush that makes the room sway in unison, conversations threading between notes like a second melody. Papà walks a measured path through donors and capos as if the marble belongs to him. Mamma glides at his side with the smile she saves for public evenings, eyes soft and careful.

Cara leans close, lips brushing my ear. "If I have to compliment one more signora's emeralds, I'm going to drown myself in the punch."

"Please don't," I murmur, keeping my gaze politely engaged on an older couple approaching Papà. "The punch did nothing to you."

"The emeralds did." Her elbow nudges my ribs. "And the men. All so proud of their watches." Her tone turns conspiratorial. "Except for that one. Over there." Her chin tips toward the far side of the hall. "I don't even notice his watch, and I'm a sinner."

The quartet slides into a new movement. I follow her cue across the crowd.

My breath stutters.

He stands near the colonnade with two other men dressed in formal black fits like sin and money. Age doesn't cling to his face the way power does. Twenty-five, maybe, but the energy wrapped around him is older—coiled, contained, the kind that makes a room correct its posture without realizing why. Mahogany hair cut clean. A shadow on his jaw that reads as deliberate, not lazy. Shoulders that make a tuxedo look like it was invented for him. The eyes—God, the eyes—are the color of volcanic glass, glossy and fathomless, catching light and hoarding it.

Donatello Romano.

I've heard the name for years in the same tones people use for storms. Papà calls him useful. Soldiers call him Il Cacciatore—The Hunter—when they think no one is listening. The stories are equal parts awe and warning. None of those stories prepared me for the way his gaze sits steady on a point in the room and makes everything else blur.

Cara's whisper vibrates against my skin. "I'd climb that man like a tree."

Heat pricks under my collarbone. "You can't say that in a room full of monache."

"They're donors' wives, not nuns," she says, wicked grin flashing. "Besides, they're thinking it too."

The two men with him—Marcello Lucchese and Faustino Romano, if I read the angle of shoulders and the careful deference right—speak without moving their mouths much. Donatello listens. Doesn't fidget. Doesn't scan for exits. Keeps his hands loose at his sides as if they already know exactly what to do if anything happens.

He turns his head a fraction.

Our gazes collide.

Everything inside me stills, then rushes forward as if that look is a current and I'm too light to anchor. It doesn't feel like being seen as much as being measured and found—not wanting, not excessive—exact. Breath slides shallow into my lungs. Nipples tighten traitorously against satin, the sudden sting hidden beneath my bodice. Thighs press together on instinct, an attempt to quiet the pulse that taps insistently low in my belly.

Cara's voice dims, then returns in a gasp. "He's looking this way."

"I know." The words scrape, dry. "Don't stare."

"I'm not staring." She absolutely stares. "You're staring. And blushing."

"Because you're saying outrageous things," I hiss, even as heat climbs to my cheeks. "Stop."

Donatello's mouth doesn't smile. The line of it softens a degree, which somehow feels louder than a grin. A single nod acknowledges me without claiming, like he just confirmed an answer to a question he'd already asked himself.

Papà moves, drawing a ring of greetings with him. We shift to follow, polite shadowing drilled into me since childhood. One soldier at the edge of our orbit leans in to murmur something into Papà's ear. His gaze flicks—first to Marcello, then to Donatello. The smallest tension threads his jaw.

"Eyes to the floor when the Lucchese boys are near," Papà says to me without moving his lips, tone silk over wire. "You're not on the market tonight."

"I didn't say I was," I whisper back.

"You don't have to say it," he replies, a father who knows where attention lands at a hundred paces. "Men like that don't share."

The music swells. Applause rises around the room as the quartet finishes the piece, giving me a moment to breathe. Cara fans her face with the program as if she could cool both of us. "All right," she says. "Tell me I'm wrong."

"You're always wrong." Denial tastes like sweet wine and

goes to my head just as quickly. My gaze refuses to behave. It returns to Donatello like a compulsion.

He speaks to Marcello, head bent enough to show the clean line of his neck above the starched collar. My mind wanders where it shouldn't, picturing the rasp of his jaw sliding against the heel of my hand, the heat of that throat under my mouth, the weight of his palm spanning my waist. Nineteen feels too young to think these things and too old to pretend I don't.

Aldo appears at my elbow like a summons. "Paolina." He offers his arm with rehearsed gallantry. "Your father said you were ready to make the rounds."

My spine stiffens at the expectation tucked inside the words. "Of course."

We circle tables draped in white, with names engraved on placards, glasses polished within an inch of their lives. Aldo shakes hands and claims minor victories in low tones, every exchange a feather he tucks into a cap I'm not sure he earned. I smile and nod and do the thing I'm supposed to do—be decorative, be agreeable, be the quiet that keeps peace.

Every few steps, the crowd parts enough to align me with the colonnade again. Donatello remains where he was, conversation shifting partners around him like a dance. He doesn't hunt around the room with his gaze. He waits for it to come to him, and of course it does. No one can teach that kind of gravity.

At the edge of a toast, our gazes snag a second time.

The surrounding sounds thin to threads. Aldo's voice keeps going, talking up someone's new car—something about cavalli and velocità—but it reaches me as if through water. Donatello's attention slides over my face like a palm not yet touching, then drops, pauses at my throat where my pulse beats, returns to my eyes. Not crude. Not even hungry. Assessed. Approved.

Claimed without claim.

Heat pools lower. A ribbon of want winds tight, shocking enough I shift my weight to hide it. Aldo notices the movement and mistakes it for discomfort in my shoes. "Sit for a minute," he tells me, concerned for optics rather than me. "You'll crease your dress if you faint."

"I won't faint." The words leave on a breath that trembles anyway.

Cara materializes with two flutes of prosecco and a grin that says she missed nothing. "Here. Hydrate with bubbles."

"Bubbles aren't hydration."

"They are tonight." She clinks my glass, then follows the line of my gaze like a cat tracking a beam of light. "Oh, bella mia. If that is what your father wants for you, take notes now and save yourself some time."

"He doesn't," I say without thinking, because the way Papà tensed proved it. "He prefers... other qualities."

"Like obedience." Humor fades from her mouth. "He wants safe and convenient."

A smile that doesn't reach my chest answers. "Something like that."

"Then you better never get caught staring," she warns lightly, though her eyes are kind. "Men like Aldo don't forgive looks aimed at men like that."

The quartet begins again, and the dance floor opens. Couples move out in polite pairs, hands positioned where chap-

erones nod. Aldo offers his hand a second time. I take it because others would notice me saying no. We step into the pattern, my body following the steps carved into me since those first stilted lessons with a neighbor's son and Mamma clapping in the doorway.

Donatello doesn't dance. He watches other people move around a center he occupies without effort, then speaks to Marcello once more. They turn together toward the doors, business pulled by an invisible wire. He passes my orbit with a buffer of bodies between us, no brush, no scent, no chance to be unreasonable.

The smallest thing happens then—so small it might be an accident. His head tilts for the length of a breath, that not-smile tipping the corner of his mouth. A single buonasera dips in the air like a bow you feel rather than see.

My heart forgets its job for two full beats.

He disappears into the corridor with the other men. The room exhales and fills the space he leaves with chatter. Aldo says something about shipping schedules and the week's carichi as if the word romance could ever be translated into freight. Cara squeezes my fingers hard enough to pull me back into my body.

When the dance ends, Aldo releases my hand with a squeeze meant to communicate possession. A ring of acquaintances closes around him. My role shrinks to the edges again. I take one last look across the room, at the space near the colonnade where he stood, then swallow the ache like a lesson.

"I saw that," she sings under her breath. "If you marry

someone else and never touch him, I'll stage an intervention. And if you do touch him, tell me everything."

"Cara." *My warning sounds weak. My insides feel weaker.*

She bumps my shoulder, wickedness returning. "At least admit your body answered. Mine did."

Admission sits hot on my tongue and settles in my chest like a secret. "Fine. It answered."

"Brava." The word is a toast and a hug. "Keep your face calm," she advises. "Put all the tempest where no one can see it."

Too late. The tempest already saw itself reflected in obsidian and decided it liked the weather.

Wanting something dangerous isn't the same as reaching for it.

When I finally drag my eyes up, Donatello is already watching me. Here and now. Obsidian eyes lock with mine. Everything inside me clenches, twists, spirals. He sees me—really sees me—not as the Corsetti daughter, not as Aldo's bride, not as the mafia pawn in lace.

Just me. Broken. Betrayed.

I realize too late my veil has slipped off my lap and pooled on the sticky floor. A white flag of surrender.

He bends, impossibly graceful for a man his size, and lifts it with careful fingers. The brush of fabric over his knuckles makes my breath stall. When he straightens, he holds it out, but he doesn't let go.

"Your veil," he murmurs, voice deep velvet wrapped around a blade. "Shouldn't waste something this pure on a man who doesn't deserve it."

My throat closes. Words stick. I manage, "How… How do you know?"

His lips tilt, not a smile, not yet. "Because I know everything Aldo does. And I know what kind of woman he doesn't deserve." His eyes flick down the length of me, the ridiculous dress, the trembling hands, then back up. "Especially you."

Heat blooms under my skin. It shouldn't. God, it shouldn't. But it does.

The glass trembles as I take another sip. Bitter, sweet, burning. My voice is a whisper. "You don't know me."

"I know enough," he says, stepping closer until his shadow swallows mine. "You cry on your wedding day. You drink alone in a bar instead of walking down the aisle. And you're smart enough to run." His fingers brush mine as he finally releases the veil. "Tell me I'm wrong."

I can't. My chest rises and falls too fast.

Instead, I stand. My skirts scrape the stool. The world tilts. I should walk away. Go anywhere but here.

But when his hand cups my elbow—steady, sure, possessive—I don't flinch. I follow.

The walk from the bar to the hotel blurs, a rush of sunlight, cobblestones, and the faint burn of Amara still coating my tongue. All I know is his hand—warm, firm, threaded through mine as if he's already claimed me. The front desk clerk dares not look our way as Donatello marches us through the lobby. By the time the suite door shuts behind us with a solid click, the entire world has narrowed to the dark heat in his eyes.

I'm pressed against the door before I can think. His chest cages mine, hard muscle under tailored wool. My veil flutters to the floor again, forgotten. His mouth crashes down on mine—demanding, consuming, dragging me into a kiss that feels like a fall I can't stop.

My gasp opens me to him. His tongue sweeps in, tangling with mine, relentless and skilled. He tastes of whiskey and sin, a dangerous alchemy that makes my knees buckle. His grip tightens at my waist, holding me up like he already knows my body belongs to him.

"I shouldn't," I whisper against his mouth, but the words tremble.

He pulls back just enough to let his obsidian gaze pin me. "You're mine, Paolina. Say it."

Heat floods my cheeks. "I… I'm yours."

A growl rumbles from his chest, vibrating through me. "Good girl."

His hands slide lower, rough palms gathering the obscene layers of tulle until his fingers skim the tops of my thighs. A whimper escapes me. No one has ever touched me like this. No one has ever *dared*.

"I need to know," I stammer, breathless. "I'm not—"

"Not what?" His lips brush my jaw, trailing heat down my throat.

My voice breaks. "Not experienced."

He freezes for a heartbeat, then curses low and filthy in Italian. His hand cups my jaw again, forcing me to meet the fire in his eyes. "Virgin." The word is half-growl, half-reverence. "*Christo.*" He presses his forehead to mine, breath harsh. "I'll make it good for you. I'll make it unforgettable. Because after tonight, you'll never belong to anyone else."

His mouth claims mine again, slower this time but no less demanding, while his hands explore every forbidden inch. He lifts me effortlessly, my skirts spilling around us as he carries me to the bed. I cling to him, my heart hammering, my body betraying me with heat pooling low and fierce.

The dress is a prison. He tears at the buttons, growling when they resist, until the bodice gives and cool air kisses my flushed skin. His eyes darken when he sees me—lace bra straining over curves I've always tried to hide.

"*Bellissima*," he rasps, reverent and raw. "Curvy as fuck. Mine to worship."

The word mine echoes as his mouth descends, teeth grazing my collarbone before sucking hard enough to mark. My gasp turns into a moan when his tongue soothes the sting. His hands cup my breasts, thumbs brushing over lace until my nipples pebble painfully.

"Donatello," I gasp, arching into him.

"Say my name like that again, bella, and I'll show you the true beast I am." His hand slips beneath the lace, fingers circling one peak before pinching lightly. Pleasure shocks through me.

My hips writhe. My body begs. He groans at the sight, as though my desire is the highest offering he's ever received.

When his mouth closes over my nipple through the lace, sucking until I cry out, I forget everything—Aldo, the church, the betrayal. There is only this man, this suite, this heat.

He strips me slowly, deliberately, until I'm laid bare on the sheets, trembling under his gaze. His suit jacket and shirt hit the floor, muscles rippling in the low light, tattoos licking up his arms like secrets written in ink.

"You're perfect," he says roughly, crawling over me, caging me in. "Made for me."

His hand trails down, over the curve of my stomach, past my trembling thighs. His fingers slip between, teasing slickness I didn't even know my body could make. "So wet for me, bella. Your body already knows who it belongs to."

The first press of his finger is slow, careful, stretching me. My back arches, a cry spilling from my throat.

"That's it. Take me. Take your Donatello."

He works me open with skill and patience, whispering filth and praise in equal measure. My body melts, hips rolling, chasing every thrust of his fingers until heat coils tight inside me.

When I shatter, it's with his name tumbling from my lips, a sobbing moan that fills the suite. He doesn't stop—his mouth claims mine again, swallowing my cries as his body shifts above me.

"Condom," I manage, breathless.

"Always prepared." He tears one open with his teeth, sheathing himself in one swift motion. Then his eyes meet mine, dark and burning. "Look at me when I take you, Paolina."

The blunt head of his cock presses against my entrance. My breath catches, body tense. His thumb strokes my cheek, gentling even as his voice roughens. "It will hurt for a moment. But I'll be your first… and your last."

He pushes slowly, stretching me wider than I thought possible. Pain and pleasure twist until I cry out. He stills instantly, eyes searching mine.

"Breathe, bella. Let me in."

I nod, clutching his shoulders, fingernails marking crescents in his skin. He moves again, inch by inch, until he seats his full length deep inside me. Full. Claimed. Branded.

The pain ebbs, replaced by a fullness so consuming I can't breathe. When he moves—long, deliberate thrusts— my body ignites. Pleasure builds again, sharper, brighter, unstoppable.

His pace quickens, hips slamming into mine. The bed creaks, my moans rise, his growls fill the suite. Each thrust drives the truth deeper: I'm his. Always his.

When I break again, it's violent, blinding, stars bursting behind my eyes. He follows with a roar, spilling into the condom as his body shudders above mine.

For a long moment, we just breathe together, tangled in sweat and silk sheets. His lips brush my temple, softer than I ever imagined Donatello Romano could be.

"You belong to me now," he whispers, final and absolute.

And though I should deny it, my heart answers before my mouth does.

Yes.

Until the haze of ecstasy clears and reality returns.

My gaze turns to the partially closed bathroom door.

Steam fogs while he showers. My body aches in places I didn't know could feel pleasure and pain at once. My heart hammers with a dangerous truth: Donatello Romano just claimed me in every way that matters.

And yet…

I stare at a leather duffel on the chair. A stack of euros spills from the half-zipped pocket, careless in its abundance. My gaze drops to the notepad on the desk. My hand trembles as I scrawl a single line:

I'll pay you back one day.

I leave the note on the nightstand. The veil too.

Then I slip into my dress and out the door, clutching the bag to my chest like it's the only lifeline I have left.

I don't look back.

CHAPTER 4

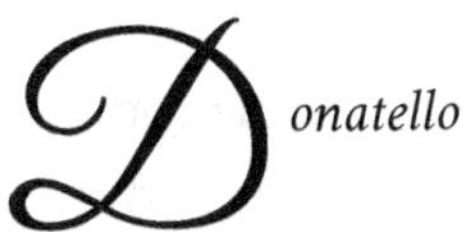onatello

STEAM GHOSTS across the bathroom mirror as I rake water from my hair. The hotel's rain shower still drums behind me, a steady hiss that should calm a man who knows how to control breath, pulse, and pain—his and other people's. It doesn't touch me. Not when the sheets on the bed are cooling around an absence shaped exactly like a woman who just became mine.

Paolina.

Her name tastes like a vow.

I drag a towel down my chest and freeze.

The nightstand holds two things: a folded veil that looks like surrendered clouds... and a note on hotel stationery written in a quick, feminine hand. I lift it between wet fingers.

I'll pay you back one day.

My jaw tightens. Not the money. Never the money. She could steal every euro I touch and still owe me nothing. The problem is the idea buried inside the sentence—the small, brave belief that there is a world where she and I aren't already inevitable.

I inhale once through my nose, tasting citrus from the bar still clinging to her hair. Bitter orange and sugar. *Amara e dolce.* That's her. Soft where I want to worship, steel where I want to test.

The towel hits the chair. My gaze sweeps the room—door chain off, latch aligned, carpet fibers crushed in a trail from bed to desk to exit. The leather duffel I dumped on the armchair gone. I picture her small hands hesitating over the zipper, the way her breath must have hitched when she saw the cash. Smart girl. A new life costs, especially when you're running from men who think they can buy everything back with blood.

I pocket the note. Then I move.

The hallway camera catches me before I make it to the elevators. Manager first. Money slides a lock open faster than keys.

Downstairs, the lobby's marble gleams under chandeliers, the kind of *vecchia signora* hotel where privacy is religion and staff pretend not to see sins if you tip them properly. I don't bother with pretense. The night manager is pale when he clocks me coming.

"Signor Romano—"

"Back office. Now."

He scurries. I follow, long strides eating carpet, suit jacket thrown on over bare chest because speed matters more than decorum, and I'm fresh from the shower and still burning. In the cramped control room, four monitors show the doors, the hall, the elevator bank, and the street. I plant a hand on the console and lean over the shoulder of the kid at the controls.

"One hour back," I say. "Guest floor twelve. Corridor B."

The kid taps. We watch grainy footage roll in reverse —housekeeping carts, a bellman ferrying luggage, a couple arguing quietly in the language of rich people who hate each other. My room's door swings open on screen, and there she is.

She pauses. Looks both ways like a little rabbit. Adjusts the burden strapped diagonally across her torso —the duffel riding high to keep from dragging. Wedding dress swallowed in the camera's gray, a hand clutched to her chest like a shield.

My throat goes tight.

She moves left. Stops. Looks right. Head tips as if she can hear me even through time and pixels telling her to run. Then she walks fast, carefully, without turning back.

"Follow," I order. The kid scrubs forward. Elevator doors open; she enters. Ground floor footage clicks on. She's smaller here, dwarfed by marble and velvet ropes. She keeps her head down, slips behind a group checking in, then drifts toward the side exit like a ghost in tulle.

Street camera picks her up next: sun at her back, city alive around her, scooters darting, an old man closing his shop's metal gate with a rattle. She lifts a hand to shield her eyes. Tulle snags on a wrought-iron bench and tears. She hesitates, bends as if to gather it, then leaves it. A bridal molting. She disappears into a narrow lane that kills the angle.

"Show me the lane," I say.

The manager wrings his hands. "No city feed there, signore."

"You have a rear service camera."

His gaze flickers. I nod once at the kid; he flips to a dusty feed. There. Paolina again cuts across a loading bay, ducking beneath the lip of a truck ramp to avoid a porter lighting a cigarette.

Smart girl. She knows how not to be seen. That means she either watched a lot of men like me, or she learned fast today. Both feed the same hunger.

The screen goes blank at the alley mouth. No more angles.

"How long ago?" I ask.

The manager licks his lips. "Forty minutes. Perhaps forty-five."

My fingers drum once against the console. She's on foot, dress hindering. Even cut from the skirting, she wouldn't clear more than a couple of yards before changing. Where would a woman go with cash, panic, and a wedding dress she needs to shed? Not to family. Not to *amici* who report to fathers and fiancés. Somewhere anonymous first—bathroom in a café, thrift shop, cheap boutique where no one asks questions if bills are crisp.

I straighten. "Copy the footage," I tell the kid. "USB. Now."

He fumbles with the port. The manager asks if he should call the police. I laugh once. "No. You'll call no one. You'll also forget this conversation. Keep forgetting, and Santa Lucia smiles on you. Remember wrong, and I don't."

He believes me. People always do.

The bar sits three corners away. The same one whose door blew a sunbeam across the floorboards ocean when I first saw her drowning at a high stool. La Sirena is busier now that the worst heat has passed. Glass clicks on wood, men talk soccer and shipping schedules, and the bartender polishes a shining curve of counter with a white towel while clocking everything reflected in the big mirror.

He recognizes me and gets smart. "*Buonasera, signore.*"

"You gave a bride a drink," I say, and lay money down without looking. "What did she say?"

His mouth barely moves. "Less with the words. More with the eyes."

"Did anyone approach her?"

He shakes his head, then stops. "A nun came in. Small. Old. Asked for a bottle of water, left with two. The bride was gone by then."

"A nun," I repeat, deadpan. He spreads hands.

"Sicily," he says, which is an answer and a shrug and a prayer in one word.

"Bathroom?"

He tips his chin toward a door. I check the single stall —clean, freshly used, paper in the bin, watermarks on the sink lip. The air smells of soap and orange blossom. I see her there: tugging stubborn buttons, breathing hard, cursing in a whisper as she fights a dress designed to make a woman feel precious and helpless in the same stitch.

Back on the street, clouds stack over Etna. Heat leaches into the stones. I dial as I walk.

Faustino answers on the first ring. "*Fratellino.*"

"Club," I say, and turn toward the villa where the wealthy go to buy whatever they cannot otherwise take. "Now."

Club Petali rises behind wrought-iron gates and cypress sentries. A Roman prince built the bones to house a mistress; the Luccheses trimmed the hedges with money and sin. The drive is long, a corridor of shade and expectation. Men study men here, everyone armed with cash and reputation. Women float in silk and intent. I ignore what usually entertains me. Tonight, the music grates, the perfume cloys, and laughter sounds like cutlery.

Security opens the doors. Crystal drips light over marble in blossoms. A maid passes with a tray of prosecco; I wave her off. The office sits beyond twin staircases, through a passage papered in velvet the color of old hearts. Two soldiers nod me in. I don't knock.

Marcello sprawls on a leather sofa, legs long, gun holstered but never far, the baby-face that makes women obey him utterly at odds with the merciless mind behind those mink brown eyes. Faustino stands by the wet bar, pouring whiskey with surgical care. He always looks carved from the same dark stone as me, only older by a year and more measured when blood runs hot.

They both turn, reading me for what a lesser man would call emotion and what my brothers—one through the bond of friendship and the other blood—recognize as fire in a steel drum.

Faustino lifts the glass like an offering. "Drink?"

I take it. It lands harshly and cleanly on my tongue, scorches down, and does nothing but gives my hands something to do. I tell them in a handful of lines what I learned, what I saw, what I intend.

Marcello whistles low. "You show a girl the sky and expect her not to try her wings," he says, dry. Then his gaze sharpens. "We'll find her."

I pace. The office is big; it still feels too small when my body wants to hunt. "I don't want eyes. I want answers."

"You'll have both," Faustino says. Calm, certain. "Give me markers to start."

"Non-family clinics for early tests," I say. "Cash rooms in cheap hotels within three miles. Shops that sell jeans and a black T-shirt at noon to a woman who looks like a runaway bride. *Tabaccai* with back-room phones. Station lockers. Bus stations. Boat charters that don't log what they should. Everyone who sprays bedding in hotel rooms and launders sheets in the quarter near Santa Maria del Carmelo. And every asshole who owes Aldo a favor; he's the kind of *coglione* who calls in favors for the wrong reasons at the wrong times."

Marcello's mouth twitches. "I'll have Rafe pull camera grids and scrape purchase logs. He loves a hunt."

"Rafe?" I repeat, and he nods toward the door.

"Raffaele Costa," Marcello says. "You call him a hacker, and he gets offended. '*Intelligence architect*,' he says, like he builds skyscrapers out of zeros." He grins a little at the memory. "He's the one who found that Bratva off-grid storage farm under *Wembley*, remember?"

"I remember," I say, because the operation ended with three Russians in a river and a crate of very pretty Glocks no longer belonging to Moscow. "Tell him it's personal. Tell him if he brings me a trail I can put my boots on, I'll buy him a new server farm and a summer house to hide it in."

Marcello is already typing. "He'll do it for the sport, fratello. But he'll take the house."

Faustino hands me a second drink. I set it down untouched. The floor hums a little under our feet—music, sex, money, a thousand appetites fed like lions in the basement. I want none of it. I want one woman. The surprise hits my ribs like a palm. I've wanted thousands of bodies. I've taken hundreds.

Desire used to be simple: pick, hunt, own for a night, leave before dawn turns the edges soft. This is not that. This is me standing in a room full of every vice I could pay to taste and aching for a stubborn Sicilian girl with lemon blossoms in her hair and a spine that wouldn't fold even when I pressed my weight on it.

Faustino sees it in my face and doesn't flinch. "She'll be afraid," he says, pragmatic as a blade.

"Maybe ashamed, because society teaches women to carry shame that belongs to men. She'll choose places where eyes slide off her."

"Good," I say, and mean it. "If the eyes slide off, they won't catch her until I do."

Marcello's phone buzzes. He glances, mouth curving. "Rafe says he's already in the municipal feeds and three private networks near the church. He also says you look like shit when you're in love."

I bare my teeth. "I look like a man who had his woman in his bed and then found air."

"You'll have her back," Faustino says simply. He lifts his chin at the door. "And there's a rat scratching."

A knock that isn't a knock. The kind that belongs to someone who mistakes familiarity for safety.

"*Entra*," Marcello calls, amusement threaded through the syllables like wire.

Aldo steps in. Smarmy in a suit. He wears a tux again tonight, no blood on it this time, face still faintly marked from the backhand I laid on him in the warehouse. The skin there probably sings when he shaves.

I hope it burns.

"Boss," he says, trying to pitch his tone to loyalty and landing on obsequious. "You wanted me?"

I turn toward him and let silence spread, a red carpet laced with razors. Then I say, "Tell me where your bride is."

His mouth does something I don't like—a curl he thinks he hides and doesn't. "My bride?" He almost laughs and swallows it at the last second when he recognizes his own stupidity. "I haven't seen Paolina since—" He stops again. Good choice. The words *since I was inside her best friend in the confessional* wouldn't do anything but get him hurt fast.

"You haven't seen her since you failed to keep her," I say. "Where is she?"

"I don't—"

"Stop," I tell him, voice flat. "Lie again, and I take things you value."

He blanches. Men like Aldo don't value truth, but they do value their tongues, their hands, the parts of themselves that make them dangerous and make women glance twice. He closes his mouth. Opens it. Shuts it again. Then throws his father-in-law under the bus because cowards always need someone to land on.

"Corsetti told me to stand down," he blurts. "Said it was *famiglia* business if she ran. Said they'd find her, and I wasn't to show my face at the church again today."

I step close enough to smell his cologne—expensive,

anise bitter, the kind boys wear to feel like men. "And did he?"

"To my knowledge?" He tries for insolence and reaches petulance. "No. She—She humiliated us. She'll come crawling back when she realizes what leaving means."

"She won't crawl." My hand closes around his tie and brings him forward until his shoes lift just enough to make his calves shudder. "But you might."

His eyes go wide. His hands stay down. He knows better than to reach for me. A muscle twitches high on his cheekbone. "With respect, signore, I had nothing to do with—"

"With my woman running?" I suggest. "You had everything to do with it. You taught her exactly what she didn't want. I should thank you." I release him with a flick that almost makes him fall.

He catches the desk with a palm, breath flaring. His gaze skitters to Marcello, then to Faustino, hunting for an ally and finding wolves who eat weaker wolves for fun. He doesn't dare question my possessive claim of his fiancée. Punk.

Marcello smiles like a winter day. "You'll go back to the warehouse, Aldo," he says, conversational. "You'll supervise the new intake, and you'll pretend you don't know why your access levels changed. If you fart out of line, the system notifies me, and my brother will practice a new kind of surgery."

"I—"

"Say *sì, Capo*," I advise.

He swallows it whole. "*Sì, Capo.*"

"*Fuori*," I add, and he's smart enough to obey.

The door closes. I roll my shoulders once, easing tension out of muscles that would prefer to break things. Faustino pours a drink he knows I won't take and leaves it, anyway.

"I want every ferry manifest in the next hour," I say, picking up the hunt again because the only cure for wanting is motion. "Every rental car lot flagged for a woman paying cash and not giving a surname. Every shop where a bride might ask for scissors."

"*Subito,*" Marcello says, already sending the order to soldiers who deal in paper and pixels instead of knives. "Rafe's building a live board. He's overlaying shop grids with our camera maps and the church's fallout radius. He just pinged a cash-only thrift on *Via Etnea* that sold denim and a black tee twenty minutes after your time-stamp. Baggy sizes. The clerk says the woman wore her hair up and paid with crisp euros. She left in a baseball cap and sunglasses with a plastic grocery bag, your duffle, and—" He pauses, reading. Then he grins. "She asked for a pair of scissors and a garbage bag."

My chest loosens a notch I didn't know had cinched tighter. "That's her," I say, certainty like a lock clicking. "She cut the dress. Bagged what remained. Shed the skin."

"Camera outside the thrift is down," Marcello adds, annoyed. "Rafe's cross-checking neighboring cams."

"Taxi ranks," Faustino says thoughtfully. "She wouldn't walk far in new shoes. She'd want out fast before anyone saw and recognized her."

"Or she stole a scooter," I say, and can't help the flash of a smile because Paolina on a stolen Vespa wearing a baseball cap and defiance is a picture that shouldn't make me hard but does. "If she did, I'll buy her three more."

Faustino's phone, quiet until now, buzzes once against the bar. He listens, grunts, and hangs up. "Two of ours at the port say a nun bought two bottles of water from La Sirena then walked toward the bus terminus."

I laugh low. "The bartender saw her too."

"Everyone sees nuns," Marcello says. "No one looks."

"She doesn't have a passport," Faustino points out. "If she heads for the airport, we'll catch her in the lobby. If she heads for *Stazione Centrale*, she disappears on a bus to Palermo or Messina."

"She won't go far," I say, and feel it in my bones like weather. "Not yet. She'll want distance before decisions. Pick a cheap room with a lock first. Buy a toothbrush. Take a shower so hot she tries to scald the feel of me off her skin and fails. She'll sit on a thin mattress with her hands on her knees and breathe until she stops shaking. Then she'll sleep like a child who ran until she fell."

"Like a woman who ran from wolves and found a cave," Marcello says, eyes gone not soft but knowing. He's hunted more than I have. He respects prey that survives.

"I am not her wolf," I say. "I am the only safe place she'll ever have."

Faustino nods once. "Then we bring her home."

Not to the compound but to my private sanctuary. The island waits, glittering under a sky so blue it hurts. A villa with a courtyard where bougainvillea climbs and a bedroom terrace set with a low bed draped in gauze the breeze can lift. A helipad hums at the far edge, boats shoulder the dock, the sea changes color with the hour. I built that place to be unreachable. Now I imagine her walking those halls barefoot, hair loose down her back, hand on her belly when she thinks no one watches. I imagine worship conducted properly—on my knees, on silk, with patience and teeth.

The desk phone trills, a shrill note that has no place in a room like this. Marcello picks it up, says nothing, listens, then slides the handset to loudspeaker.

Rafe's voice comes through tinned and pleased. "Got your girl's cap on camera crossing into *Via Pacini*," he announces. "Face half turned, but the timestamp is eight minutes after the thrift. She cut through the market, bought a cheap canvas duffel, and disappeared into *Vicolo degli Angeli*—most cameras blind there. But she emerges three minutes later in trainers, not pumps. Baseball cap, sunglasses, black tee, denim. Dress is gone. She heads south. Loses herself in the *Viale della Libertà* flow."

"Bus terminus?" Faustino asks.

"Negative. She stops at *Hotel Mirto*. Three-star, cash friendly. No bags when she arrives—just the grocery sack. Ten minutes later, a maid exits with a black garbage bag knotted tight and tosses it in the alley dumpster. Want me to pull it?"

"I already am," I say, and look at my brother. "Who's closest?"

"Leone," Marcello answers immediately. "He and Bruno are two blocks off. They'll knock on the side door and ask for the manager like gentlemen."

"Have them go as ghosts," I counter. "No conversations. We don't spook her. Pull the dumpster bag, verify what's inside, tag the room number from the maid's cart schedule, set a camera on the corridor, then fall back and wait. She sleeps; we watch. She leaves; we follow. No one touches her but me."

Faustino's mouth curves. "*Capito.*"

Marcello relays. Rafe hums like a kid at Christmas. "Copy."

"Good," I say.

"You're assuming she comes quietly," Marcello says, but he doesn't mean quietly as much as he means willingly.

"I'm assuming she comes," I answer, and feel the calm that only arrives when a plan and a desire click. "I took her virginity; now I take responsibility. She'll hate the word *marriage* until I teach her a different definition. She'll hate the word *possession* until she understands it means *protection* when it comes from me. And she'll learn *love* isn't a weakness when a man like me kneels to it."

Faustino pours the drink he knew I'd need after all.

This time I take it, not for the burn, but for our ritual. We drink to beginnings and endings in rooms like these. Tonight is both.

The door opens without a knock—again—and Leone slides in, efficient, breath barely raised. He sets a black garbage bag on the floor. "From the *Mirto* alley," he reports. "Housekeeping chart says they serviced Room 214. The maid's name is Giovanna. Twenty-four minutes between her going in and coming out."

I slit the tie. Layers of fabric spill like a corpse made of lace. A bodice with pearl buttons ripped from its seams. Skirt cut in angry, clean strips. A satin shoe with the heel broken and blood on the strap where it blistered skin.

My body goes silent.

Marcello watches me. "That's your proof she's still bleeding," he says, unsentimental. "Not from you. From the day."

I nod once. "She'll rest now."

"Room 214?" Faustino confirms with Leone. He nods. I picture the *Mirto's* corridor—faded runner, brass numbers screwed crooked into doors, a housekeeping cart squatting like a fat dog outside one. Paolina inside behind a lock she believes can stop the world. Her breathing calming, her fingers unclenching one by one, a shower washing sugar and sin off skin, the curls at her nape frizzing in cheap steam. A bed that is not mine holding her lush body safe for a few hours.

"Two on the exits," I say. "One watches the desk. I'll take the rest."

Marcello lifts a brow. "You going to sit in a lobby chair and read a newspaper like a husband who forgives?"

"I'm going to sit where she can't see me and listen to the sound the elevator makes when it stops on the second floor." I look at them both. "When she comes down, she'll meet me, or she'll meet the day. I prefer that she meets me."

Faustino tosses me a key fob. "S-Class out front. You won't drive it far."

"I won't drive it at all," I say, and tuck the veil from the hotel into my jacket pocket because I took the note and I take the symbol. "When she sees me, she'll run. I'll let her. Once. She needs to learn what it feels like to be chased by a man who never stops."

Marcello chuckles. "You're a romantic, fratello."

"I'm a hunter," I correct. Then I set the empty glass down with a soft click. "And I'm done waiting."

The *Mirto* sits in the shadow of *Viale della Libertà*, a dowdy three-story building that pretends it was elegant once and knows it wasn't. I park half a block away, walk past a newsstand that peddles lottery tickets and magazines featuring actresses with impossible lips, and nod to a woman watering geraniums on a balcony. Inside, the lobby smells of lemon cleaner and old air-conditioning. A fan ticks at the ceiling. The clerk at the desk looks up, eyes widening, then dropping, survival instincts quicker than fear.

I don't speak to him. A cracked leather chair in the corner faces the elevator and a wall mirror angled to catch the stairwell. I sit. People become invisible fastest when they act like they belong. Kings and thieves know this trick equally well.

Time lengthens. The mirror shows me distorted, taller, the way carnival glass makes men into myths. Footsteps scrape upstairs, slow and tired. The elevator hums, stops on three, goes nowhere, grinds back to two. A maid's cart squeaks. Somewhere a TV plays a soap opera argument dripping with betrayal and wild violins.

The elevator shudders, opens, and breathes out a woman in a black T-shirt and denim, baseball cap low, sunglasses oversized, a canvas duffel slung across her chest like a shield, trainers silent. She looks left, then right. Her chin lifts, a small, stubborn tilt I want to kiss. Blood dried like a thin necklace across the top of her foot where the strap cut earlier; she put the trainers on too fast for socks. It makes me love her more.

She doesn't see me. Instead, her eyes track the door. She walks. Her hand brushes the desk, a ghost tip that leaves two keys she doesn't want to need again.

Just before she reaches the threshold, wind bellies the awning outside and the street noise swells—voices, the pop of a scooter backfiring, an old man laughing, the click of a woman's heels. It distracts her for a fraction of a second. She decides in that second to look back.

Her eyes hit the mirror first. Then they ricochet to me.

Everything in the room goes still.

Her breath stops. Mine doesn't. I rise without hurry because speed is for prey, and I am not prey.

"Paolina," I say, and my voice comes out quiet and certain, the way a tide speaks when it takes a shore. "Come."

She makes the only choice she can make: the one that proves she's exactly the woman I already decided to spend the rest of my life chasing. She bolts.

Out the door, into the late afternoon, down the steps in one flying leap, cap tightening with the force of motion. I let her go, count three heartbeats because I promised myself I would, then I follow.

Hunt begins.

CHAPTER 5

5 Months Later — New York City
Paolina

THE BELL above the diner door jingles, another gust of January wind knifing through before it slams shut. I tuck the pencil behind my ear, balancing a tray with one hand, and paste on the smile I save for customers who think I'm too young or too soft to handle their complaints.

The Formica counter shines with the same greasy sheen as my apron. The smell of frying bacon and burnt coffee seeps into my skin until I swear it comes out of my pores. Plates clatter. Voices rise and fall. A toddler shrieks in delight as her father flips her a sugar packet like it's treasure.

This isn't what Papà imagined for his daughter. Not a Corsetti heiress. Not the girl who used to glide through ballrooms under crystal chandeliers, arm locked with Aldo's, pretending she wanted the life chosen for her.

But I'd rather be a fallen mafia princess slinging hash in Queens than the wife of Aldo Buratti.

I set down the tray with three burgers, balancing it with the grace drilled into me from etiquette classes. "Order up," I call, sliding ketchup bottles across the table. "Anything else?"

The men grunt, already devouring. My smile fades before I turn. My back aches from the long shift, but the five months double the ache growing inside me. The uniform does little to hide the swell of my belly now. Some customers give me the soft looks reserved for mothers. Others give me the sharper looks meant for scandal.

I learned not to care.

The baby shifts. A flutter against my ribs, gentle and insistent. My hand presses low to calm us both.

Donatello's baby.

Heat creeps into my cheeks at the thought of him, uninvited, but always there. It should be shame. But it's not. It's the way my body still remembers his weight, his mouth, his voice saying my name like a vow.

I don't let myself linger. My survival depends on moving forward, not drowning in what already claimed me.

Still, sometimes my mind betrays me. It slips back to that day in the hotel lobby—only hours after I'd run from his bed.

My heart still thundered from leaving the veil, the note, and the man.

The hotel lobby's marble glistened. I remember freezing at the sight of him near the elevators, jaw shadowed, shirt fresh, eyes scanning the crowd. He was there. Hunting. For me.

"Paolina, come."

Instinct took over. I bolted.

I ducked behind a German tour group, slipped out the side entrance, cut through alleys I knew from childhood like veins. I never looked back. Not until the bus roared toward Palermo, and I dared to glance through the dirty window, heart hammering, waiting for his obsidian eyes to find me.

They didn't.

I bought a new passport and a new name from a man who didn't blink at cash thick enough to choke a horse. Money gets you anything, especially in Sicily if you know which shadows to knock on.

From Palermo, a flight to Paris. From Paris to five months later, I'm *Maria Rossi*, waitress, American transplant with a questionable accent and swollen belly.

I think of Mamma, and how she'd fuss over me and the baby. The thought twists something sharp in my chest.

The night I left Sicily, I bought a burner phone with cash from Donatello's duffel. Just one message. Just enough.

I'm safe. I love you. But I'm not coming back. I can't marry Aldo. I won't face Papà's anger. Don't look for me.

I deleted it after I hit send, tossed the phone out the window as the bus pulled away.

I imagine her reading it in the kitchen, maybe clutching the counter for balance, maybe weeping in silence so Papà doesn't hear. The guilt claws at me. But the alternative—going back to Aldo or facing Papà's fury —would have been worse.

Better a daughter gone than a daughter broken.

I wipe down the counter, forcing myself back into the present.

The shift ends after dark. The manager barely nods as I hang my apron on the hook, trading the smell of grease for the stale cold air of the street. My sneakers slap against pavement wet with melted snow. Neon signs buzz, taxis honk, and I clutch my worn coat tighter around my middle as I climb three flights of stairs to my studio.

It isn't much. A single room that smells faintly of mildew no matter how many lavender-scented candles I burn. A rickety bed. Used hot plate. A cracked window. But it's mine. Mine and my baby's.

The door clicks shut behind me. I lock both deadbolts out of habit, drop my bag, and rub my swollen feet.

Then the light snaps on.

A scream rips out of me. My heart slams against my ribs.

He sits in the chair by the window, legs spread, hands

clasped loosely, like a king on a throne he didn't even need to build. His presence swallows the room whole.

"W—What are you doing here?" My voice breaks into staccato. "How did you find me?"

Donatello scoffs, rising to his full, terrifying height. "*La bestia alla tua bellezza.* The beast to your beauty."

The nickname slithers around me, a noose made of velvet. My hand flies to my belly as if my palm could shield my baby from the weight in his voice.

His eyes flash. Not just dark obsidian—alive, molten, lethal. "Did you really think you could run from me, *bella mia*? Did you think you could keep *my* child from me?"

Tears sting my lashes. My heart ricochets. I back up until my spine collides with the door with nowhere left to go.

"Donatello—" My plea a hoarse whisper.

He stalks closer, every step measured, deliberate, until his shadow swallows mine. His hand presses against the door above my head, caging me without even touching. "You thought you could leave Sicily. Leave *me*. Disappear. Carry my baby. Tell me, Paolina—" His voice drops, deadly quiet. "—what kind of fool do you take me for?"

My lip trembles. "I—I only wanted—"

"You wanted to survive," he cuts in, sharp. "But survival without me is suicide. And you know it."

His other hand drops suddenly, cupping the curve of my stomach. My breath seizes. The baby kicks as if answering him. His jaw flexes, nostrils flaring.

"My child," he growls, reverence tangled with possession. "Our child."

"Please—" My hands flutter uselessly. "I can't—I don't—"

"You don't what?" He leans closer, his breath brushing my cheek. "Don't want me? Don't want this?"

His thumb strokes over the swell beneath my shirt, slow and deliberate. "Then why does your body still answer mine, bella? Even now."

Tears spill hot. I shake my head. "I can't go back."

"You're not going back." His lips curve in something crueler than a smile. "You're going forward. With me. Always with me."

The decision is already made. It always is.

He steps back, hand gripping mine before I can resist. He grabs the small bag where I keep my prenatal vitamins, tucks it under his arm. "You take these. Nothing else. Everything else you need—I provide."

"Donatello—"

"No, Paolina." His tone silences me. "No more running. No more lies. You are mine. The baby is mine. *La famiglia* is mine. And now, so are you."

I stumble as he guides me out the door. He straightens me with ease and continues down the stairs, into the night. A black SUV idles at the curb, sleek and gleaming in the moonlight. A man in a suit opens the door.

My gaze darts around. Dare I call for help? Would my neighbors dare to intervene?

As if reading my thoughts of escape, Donatello crushes the thought with his grip. His lips hover near my ear, breath burning across my skin.

"Don't even try it, Paolina. Your days of running are finished."

He doesn't release me until we're inside. The city blurs past in streaks of neon and shadow. My breath hitches when a private airfield appears.

The Gulfstream waits like a dark-winged predator. Steps lower, lights glow softly inside. He doesn't let go until I'm buckled into a leather seat. My bag disappears into a storage bin. His hand returns to mine, possessive and grounding.

The engines roar. My body trembles. Adrenaline drains, leaving exhaustion in its place. My little one moves, probably just as drained as me. I place a calming hand on my belly.

"Are you hungry?"

The question scrapes across my nerves. The thought of eating knots my stomach tighter. My insides feel like a coiled fist. I shake my head and close my eyes, as if shutting out the world will silence him too.

"You don't look good," he murmurs, more observation than sympathy. "You've lost weight when women gain during pregnancy. The doctor will check you. I'll make sure you—and our baby—are healthy."

A sigh is all I can manage—part defiance, part surrender.

Donatello grunts, the sound low and disapproving, like he already knows my silence is temporary.

The engines drone a steady lullaby, and exhaustion drags me under. Sleep claims me despite the fear twisting in my chest.

Mid-flight, he wakes me and leads me into the bedroom suite, a cocoon of cream leather and silk bedding. I sink onto the mattress, too drained to argue, too tired to resist. My eyes flutter.

The last thing I feel is his hand smoothing over my belly again, protective and terrifying all at once.

"You're safe, *bella mia.* You and our baby are safe."

Darkness takes me.

I startle awake at the shift of the mattress beside me.

Donatello is up, broad shoulders outlined against the cabin's muted glow. He stands at the window, head bowed slightly, one hand braced against the frame, the other raking through his hair. For a moment I wonder if he's wrestling with himself the way I am—with choices, with chains neither of us asked for.

Then he turns, and the storm in his eyes tells me whatever battle rages in him, it won't change one thing.

Donatello kept his promise. I'm his. And there's no escape.

 aolina

"WE'VE LANDED."

I straighten, hand instinctively bracing my stomach. "Where are we?"

"You'll see."

Two words. Nothing more.

The cabin door opens, cool sea air rushing in. It carries salt and jasmine, a softness at odds with the iron grip that closes around my arm as he guides me down the steps. The tarmac gives way to a sleek helipad where a black helicopter waits, blades thumping impatiently.

Fear claws my chest. "Another flight? Donatello, I—"

"Shhh." His hand presses to the small of my back, steady but inescapable. "It's short."

The helicopter swallows us. Darkness cloaks the world outside as we rise. I cling to the seat belt, nerves frayed. Donatello watches me without blinking, every inch the predator guarding his prize. The baby shifts, unsettled, and I murmur soft nonsense under my breath, trying to calm both of us.

Ten minutes later, a jeweled horizon appears: an island rising from black water, its edges traced in golden light. Villas with wall sconces gleam like pearls nestled amongst up-lit flowering trees and manicured lawns. Additional landscape lighting marks the paths between the villas and recreation areas. A grass tennis court, a pool glimmering turquoise even at night with its cabana flanked by chaise lounges, and a boat dock lined with sleek yachts and jet skis round out the resort feel. In the center, a courtyard spilling with fuchsia and purple bougainvillea and teak seating areas offer sanctuary. A stunning paradise, despite the patrols of armed men.

My breath catches. "Where are we?"

"My island." His tone holds no arrogance, only fact. "Your home now."

The helicopter settles on the villa's helipad. Staff waits—two men in dark suits, a woman in white, another man with a doctor's bag. They move with quiet efficiency, bowing their heads as Donatello leads me towards them.

The primary villa towers, all pale stone and sweeping arches, lanterns casting honeyed light over carved balconies. My sneakers whisper against polished marble as he steers me inside past a pair of sentries.

It's too much. Too beautiful. Too… trapped.

The atrium opens around us, ceilings soaring, chandeliers glittering like captured starlight. The scent of ylang-ylang and salt water lingers in the air. For a heartbeat I almost forget myself, caught in the spell of opulence. Then his hand tightens, reminding me I'm not a guest.

I'm a possession. His possession.

"You can't keep me here." The words escape sharper than I intend.

"I can," he replies smoothly, eyes narrowing. "And I will."

I whirl to face him, chin lifted despite the tremble in my knees. "Donatello—this is kidnapping."

"No." His large hand frames my jaw, thumb brushing my cheek with deceptive gentleness. "This is protection. For you. For *our* child. You think the world outside would give you safety? Aldo would let you live after you embarrassed him? Your father's wrath would spare you?" His grip tightens. "Here, no one can touch you. Here, you are mine."

The word burns through me—mine—both terrifying and shamefully thrilling.

"I don't want this," I whisper.

"You don't know what you want yet." His gaze hardens to obsidian. "But by the time my daughter is born, you'll love me. That's my vow."

A shudder rolls through me. "You can't force my love."

"Can't I?" He tilts his head, lips curving in a smile that isn't kind. "I've already taken your fear, your body, your flight. Love is next. And I'll make sure when you give it, it's because you've learned the truth: no one else will ever worship you as I do."

Tears sting my eyes, but I blink them back. "You don't know me."

"I know enough." His hand drops to my belly, spreading warm and firm across the swell. The baby shifts as if recognizing his touch. His voice lowers, husky and certain. "And what I don't know yet, I'll learn. Every sigh, need, secret. You'll give them all to me."

I step back, desperate for space. "You can't buy me."

"Not with money," he says simply, then rubs my belly. "I already own you with something greater."

I can't breathe.

He turns, issuing commands in rapid Italian to the staff. The woman in white—clearly a nurse—steps forward. The doctor follows, murmuring about prenatal checkups and supplements.

"No," I snap, backing up. "You can't—"

Donatello's hand settles heavy on my shoulder. "Yes. The doctor will examine you. You've lost weight when women gain during pregnancy. You'll eat, rest, and be healthy. No arguments, Paolina."

I choke on fury. "And if I refuse?"

His eyes flash, dark fire. "You won't. Because it's not

just you anymore. It's *her*. And before I let you risk my daughter, I'll lock you in my bedroom instead of allowing you to roam free here."

My knees weaken. He catches me, guiding me to a velvet chair like I'm fragile glass. The doctor kneels beside me, gentle, efficient, while Donatello looms close enough I can't forget who orchestrates every second.

When they finish, he dismisses them with a flick of his fingers. Only we remain.

"You took my phone," I whisper.

"Of course." He sits across from me, sprawling in the chair like a king. "No calls, texts, or begging for rescue that will never come."

"I don't want your money. I'll pay you back."

He leans forward, elbows on his knees, gaze drilling into me. "You owe me nothing but yourself. And that, bella, I'll take in full."

My heart races, torn between fear and the shameful thrum of want.

His hand rises, cupping my cheek again. "Fight me, Paolina. Scratch, bite, run. It only makes the hunt sweeter. But when you finally give in—and you will—I'll be there. And you'll know you've always belonged here."

His thumb strokes over my lower lip, possessive, final.

I want to scream. Weep. Give in.

Instead, I whisper the only truth I dare: "I hate you."

His smile sharpens, satisfied. "Good. Hate first. Love after. Both bind you to me."

He rises, towering over me, and gestures toward the staircase that curves up into shadow. "Come. You'll see our rooms. Rest while you can, *bella mia*. The island is yours… but the world outside is gone."

My legs move because his will directs them. Marble stairs rise as the villa stretches above, magnificent and gilded. But every step feels like a door locking shut behind me.

When I reach his suite—four-poster bed dressed in white silk, balcony overlooking endless sea—I know the truth.

I am no longer running.

I am caught.

And Donatello Romano intends to make sure I never want to escape again.

"How long will you be gone?"

The question slips out before I can swallow it. It hangs in the sun-washed bedroom between the open balcony doors and the suitcase he hasn't zipped. Salt air spills through gauzy curtains, carrying the faint thrum of the Mediterranean Sea below the cliffs and the citrus note of lemons from the grove.

Two months on this island have taught me the rhythm of Donatello's life. He comes. He goes.

Business draws him away overnight, sometimes until dawn, always back before the sun has the nerve to set without him. I stay. Staff tends to me like a queen who never asked for a crown—fresh fruit on silver trays, meals tailored to cravings I don't admit out loud, appointments I never book appearing on a discreet schedule. The obstetrician checks me every week; the nurse visits daily with a calm smile and a blood-pressure cuff. Morning swims smooth the weight from my hips while the baby rolls like a sleepy dolphin in my rounded belly. The pool glitters. The Med welcomes me with cool hands. Afterward, the spa/fitness pavilion claims the hours between lunch and dusk with prenatal massage that loosens the ache beneath my shoulder blades and low-impact yoga and Pilates. All done and taught by trained professionals.

Aside from the kidnapping, Donatello has been good to me. That is a dangerous truth to admit, even in the privacy of my head. No sex. Not once. At night he pulls me into him, and we sleep locked together, his hand splayed across the round of my belly as if he can cradle the baby through skin and bone. Sometimes the length of him hardens along my backside; sometimes the restraint in his body feels like the loudest thing in the room. He never moves beyond holding me. Even though he always could, he doesn't. The absence breeds want like heat breeds storms.

I haven't spoken to Mamma. The burner phone lies crushed on a road somewhere. Papà's anger is a door I refuse to open even in memory. Silence is mercy—distance, survival.

Donatello pauses with his watch in his hand. Dark eyes flick to my face, reading more than I say. "A few days."

A few days. It hits harder than it should. This will be the first time he's gone longer than a night.

Surprise blooms into something lonelier than I expect, an ache that starts low and widens until I have to press my palm there to catch it.

"I'll manage," I say, because pride is a habit that learned to walk before love knew how to crawl.

"You will," he agrees, not as a question. He sets the watch on his wrist, then steps in to brush a thumb beneath my eye as if he can smooth the sleeplessness away. "Nora will stay close. The doctor is on call. Security is the same. Swim only when the flags are green. Eat more in the morning. Rest after dinner." His mouth softens at the corners. "And text me when you want me. I'll answer."

"Bossing me from the sky now?" It comes out lighter than I feel.

"Yes." The word is simple. Then he adds, "And because I want to kiss you before I go."

He doesn't wait for permission. Naturally. Lips find mine, warm and steady, a promise pressed into a goodbye.

The kiss is not hunger. It's claim and comfort and a thousand things I'm not ready to name. My fingers curl in his shirt, anyway. The baby rolls and stills, as if listening.

When he draws back, I breathe him in once more. "Let me walk you."

The silk kimono waits draped over the chair—cream with a scatter of painted cranes. I slide my arms through, tie the belt over a belly that has outgrown denial. Seven months and every step reminds me I'm carrying a world inside my body. He watches me knot the sash, something like pride moving beneath the iron in his gaze.

He takes my hand as we leave the suite. Marble cools the soles of my feet. The villa sighs around us—lanterns dimmed for morning, a maid's cart ghosting past a corridor, the scent of espresso whispering from the kitchen. On the terrace, bougainvillea throws fuchsia shadows across the stone. The path to the helipad slices through citrus trees heavy with fruit. He turns there, at the angle where I always stop, and he always assesses distance with a soldier's eye.

I place a hand on his arm, suddenly not wanting him to leave.

"Be careful," I whisper.

"Always. I'll be back before you count too many sunsets," he says, and the line should make me roll my eyes. It doesn't. It lands and settles like a pebble tossed into a still pool, ripples spreading.

My hand lifts without thinking. I wave. He hesitates, then does the thing that undoes me. A small, private smile meant only for me. One last look, and he's walking —dark suit cutting through green, shoulders squared for leaving. Rotor blades begin their slow thunder. Wind tears the scent of him from the air and flings my hair across my face. I hold the kimono closed and stand there until the helicopter shrinks to a black insect and then to nothing at all.

The villa is too quiet when I come back inside. Silence folds around me like a heavy robe. Loneliness pricks and sparks into restlessness fast.

A shower first. Maybe heat can rinse want from skin.

Steam fogs the mirrors. Water thunders against travertine, a bright white noise that drowns thought. I brace one hand on the wall and let the other map the territory that used to be only mine—the curve of belly, the slope of hip, the place where my pulse beats faster under my own touch. A sigh slips out before I can catch it. Closing my eyes makes it worse. He is everywhere when I shut out the world. The weight of his palm on my stomach at midnight, the rasp of his morning stubble against the nape of my neck, the inaudible murmur of *bella mia* when he thinks I'm asleep.

Fingers slide lower. Heat flares. I chase relief the way drowning lungs chase air—greedy, grateful, unpretty. The rhythm builds quickly in the shower's rush, tightens, crests. Pleasure spills through me in soft, shaking waves, water carrying the sound from my mouth away before it can embarrass me.

Afterward, I lean my forehead against the cool tile and breathe until my heart remembers a calmer beat. It isn't enough. It never is when the wanting is a man and not a moment.

Clothes, then movement. A walk might unknot what the water didn't.

I choose a soft dress that forgives the swell, sandals that won't argue with stairs, a straw hat to shade what the sun has started to love too hard. The guard at the gatehouse nods without intruding as I slip down the stone steps that spill toward the sea. The path is fragrant with rosemary and thyme, the scent that makes recipes whisper in the back of my brain even though the chef sends up meals before I can think to ask. Gulls wheel. The horizon pulls and pulls until I give in and stop.

The sea is an animal breathing. It throws light like jewels in rough hands. Waves cuff the rocks and foam in lace that never repeats itself. Far below, the private dock rocks gently under the tethered kiss of a black Riva with chrome teeth.

Seven months. Two more until the world tilts on its axis and never tips back. My palm rides the rise and fall of my belly. "What do we do, *piccola?*" I ask the wind because it's the only thing here that answers without words. "Do we marry your father because it's easier and safer and something in me has started to want the thing I swore I wouldn't? Or do we run again because freedom is a religion I don't know how to stop worshipping?"

A lemon drops somewhere up the slope with a soft thud, as if the island itself throws its hands up. I laugh once—small, surprised, not unhappy.

One life sits behind me in a villa made of stone and power and a man who holds me like home and like possession. Another life waits beyond the line where sky kisses water and boats vanish into possibility.

The past curls its fingers, the future cocks its head, and the present balances on my rib cage with the weight of a sleeping child.

For now, I stand between them and let the view take me. The choice can wait until the baby arrives, until my body is mine again or his again or something holy and complicated that belongs to all three of us. For now, the sun warms my shoulders, the sea answers in blue, and the island breathes with me as if we share lungs.

"*Andiamo, amore,*" I whisper to the tiny life inside. "Let's walk."

 aolina

THE VILLA IS SO quiet this time of morning I can hear the cicadas from the olive groves. I smooth the skirt of my maxi dress, tie a silk scarf around my hair, and make my way toward the pavilion where Nora scheduled today's Pilates session.

The path to the pavilion winds through the colonnade, sun spilling in golden shafts between arches of pale stone. The island is impossibly beautiful—bougainvillea trailing in fuchsia curtains, lemon trees heavy with fruit, the sea glittering far below like shards of sapphire. It's tranquil in a way I never imagined life could be.

I slow when I see Alberto, the gardener, crouched

among the roses. His hands stained with soil, his straw hat tilted to keep off the sun. He glances up, face creased with a smile and offers me a small basket. Inside, peaches glow, warm from the vine.

"For you, signorina," he says softly.

"Thank you." I press a hand to my belly. "She thanks you, too."

He chuckles, tapping his heart. "Always the best for you." He gestures toward the bouquet waiting on the low stone wall—gardenias and lilies, tied neatly with twine. "For your rooms."

I take the flowers, inhaling their sweetness. His careful arrangements, fresh blossoms always brighten my suite in every vase. It almost feels like home. Almost.

"I'll put everything inside for you, signorina."

"Thank you, Alberto." I smile kindly and wave.

Walking on, I can't deny the truth. If not for the kidnapping and being held in gilded captivity, this island would be paradise. A place to breathe. A place to raise a child in beauty and safety.

But the knowledge that he stole me here hovers like an ominous cloud. No matter how soft the sheets or how sweet the fruit, I can't forget.

Halfway down the colonnade, I pause.

Donatello.

He doesn't see me, and I don't dare call his name. He's on the patio, shirtless, wearing nothing but black gym shorts that hang low on his hips. Muscles ripple down his chest and arms as he lifts heavy free weights in the raw Sicilian sun. Sweat runs in rivulets, tracing over olive skin pulled tight over every hard line of him.

Most men with his money prefer air-conditioned gyms, sleek chrome machines, personal trainers who coddle them. Not Donatello Romano. He takes the punishment head-on. Iron. Stone. Sweat. He is all man, forged in the heat of this land, every rep another reminder he's a La Cosa Nostra enforcer built for violence.

And yet—when his hands touch me, when his voice drops low in the dark—he is gentle.

My thighs press together before I can stop them. Pregnancy hormones, I scold myself, heat climbing through my chest. Everything is sharper now—every glance, every brush of his body against mine at night when he holds me. Desire blooms quicker, harder. *Madonna*, it's embarrassing.

Confusion tangles with the want. How can I ache for the same man who kidnapped me? Who tore me from my life, from my mother, from every choice I thought I had?

I wish I had a friend to talk to. Someone who could tell me if it's normal to feel this—anger and longing tangled so tightly they choke me.

A snort escapes me. A friend. Cara used to be that. And look how that turned out—my so-called best friend spread beneath Aldo's body in the confessional while I stood outside like a fool.

"Signorina?"

A polite cough startles me. I turn to find my Pilates instructor waiting by the studio doors, towel slung over her arm. Her smile is professional, but her eyes—oh, her eyes—slide past me, flare hot, then linger on Donatello's glistening back.

Something ugly twists inside me. Jealousy. Possessiveness.

"He's busy," I say, voice sharp as glass. "Shall we? Or do you have other plans?"

Color rises in her cheeks as she stammers, "Of course... I mean no, signorina."

I lift my chin, holding my head high like a queen, and sweep past her into the studio, pretending the jealousy didn't rattle me to my core. Once in the changing room, I sag against the wall, covering my eyes with a hand. *Get it together, Paolina.*

I let the mixed emotions shed from my mind as I take off my dress and pull on leggings and a matching sports bra. With a nod to my reflection in the mirror, I head to the Cadillac.

The instructor is overly polite and attentive. Good. I do not regret my snarky response.

After the session, my muscles hum pleasantly. I shower in the spa, scrubbing away sweat and frustration, then slip into my dress. It stretches comfortably over my belly, soft against my skin.

I'm stepping into the corridor when a door opens across the way.

Donatello emerges from the men's changing room, hair damp, droplets running down his temple. His handsome face flushed from exertion, olive skin warm with color. When his gaze finds me, it's like the rest of the hall disappears.

"Would you like breakfast?" His voice is low, certain.

I blink, caught off guard. "Yes."

He extends his hand. I hesitate only a second before placing mine in his. His palm is warm, and his grip steady. He raises his phone, calling the chef. "Whatever she wants," he orders. Then, looking at me, he asks, "What will it be, *bella mia?*"

"Um…" I clear my throat. "Fruit. Eggs. Toast."

He nods once. "You'll have it."

We walk together to the courtyard, sunlight dappling the stones. He asks, "How was your session?"

"Good," I say, then flush. "Not as… intense as your workout."

Heat floods my cheeks as I realize I've betrayed myself—I was watching him. His chuckle is low, rich.

He squeezes my hand. "I'm glad you noticed."

My heart flutters.

The chef's staff delivers plates, steam curling from eggs, fruit sliced into gleaming jewels. We eat slowly, talking in low voices about nothing and everything— how the sea looked this morning, how strong the baby's kicks have become, how he prefers black coffee to espresso.

When we're finished, I lean against the pillows in the shaded corner of the courtyard. The sun is warm, the fountain trickles, and for a moment it feels... normal. Breakfast with a man. Talking. Smiling.

Except I'm not free. I've been kidnapped. Forced to stay. The contradiction coils tight inside me, a knot I can't untangle. And no one to talk to.

We slip into a comfortable silence. Bees buzz, flitting from one fragrant flower to the next. A koi splashes its tail in the fountain. Waves slap against the cliffs. Serenity.

Sleep pulls at me before I realize I've drifted sideways.

When I wake, it's to the sensation of being lifted. Donatello's arms cradle me against his chest. I blink up at him, groggy.

"Rest," he murmurs.

His arms are solid around me, steady as stone, and I can't stop the little sigh that slips out. For a moment I let myself melt into him, cheek against his chest, breathing in the clean scent of soap still clinging to his skin.

Aldo could never have carried me like this. Not my full, voluptuous body. He would've mocked me, set me down halfway across the room with some cutting remark about my curves. Donatello doesn't even flinch. He carries me from the courtyard all the way through the villa as if I weigh nothing, as if holding me is the most natural thing in the world.

If I close my eyes, I can almost pretend this is normal.

That I'm not a prisoner. That I'm just a woman being carried to bed by the man she loves.

And it feels… good. Too good.

Once inside the suite, Donatello sets me gently on my feet. His hands linger on my hips, large and firm, anchoring me in place. He stares down at me with an expression I can't read—dark, intent, unreadable, as though a hundred thoughts war behind those obsidian eyes.

Then his fingers curl in the fabric of my dress, bunching it at my thighs, dragging it higher. My breath catches, heat flaring through me. He lifts it over my head in one smooth pull, leaving me bare in the lamplight's glow. My heart hammers. For one wild moment I think —no, I *know*—he's about to fuck me, finally, and my body aches with the want of it.

But he doesn't.

Instead, he turns away, pulls the bedding back, and guides me down with unexpected gentleness. He helps me into the cool sheets, tucking the covers around me with the same care a man might use with glass. A hand smooths over my hair before he takes the chair in the corner, broad shoulders bent, eyes fixed on me. Watching. Guarding. Always protecting. Always there.

Disappointment burns low in my belly, shameful and sharp. I wanted him. God help me, I still want him.

I squeeze my eyes shut and chide myself. He kidnapped me. I shouldn't crave his touch, his heat, his weight pinning me down. Especially when I don't know if I want to run from him—or to him.

But as the mattress cradles me and his shadow lingers at the bedside, I can't stop the thought from whispering through me.

Maybe it would be easier if he had.

CHAPTER 8

onatello

THE SUN HASN'T BURNED off the mist yet when I button my shirt and shrug on my jacket. The air still tastes of night, cool and damp with salt. Beyond the grove, the helicopter waits, blades slack for now.

She's already awake when I step into our suite's sitting room, bringing my watch to my wrist. Paolina sits near the balcony, hair loose over her shoulders, a silk nightgown covering her belly. Seven months pregnant, glowing with a softness that makes my chest ache. She doesn't even know what she does to me.

"How long will you be gone?" she asks quietly.

"A few days."

Her lips press together, eyes lowering to the swell of her belly. "I'll manage."

"You will," I say as my thumb brushes her gorgeous face. "Nora will stay close. The doctor is on call. Security is the same. Swim only when the flags are green. Eat more in the morning. Rest after dinner. And text me when you want me. I'll answer."

"Bossing me from the sky now?"

"Yes. And because I want to kiss you before I go."

She tastes of heaven and home. I hold back a hungry groan as she melts into me.

"Let me walk you," she sighs as though the kiss means as much to her as it does to me.

I clasp her hand, never wanting to let it go.

As has become habit, we stop on the path to the helipad. I glance around, scanning for any threat, although none can reach her here. I turn to go, but her hand—small, warm—touches my arm. Light. Barely there. Enough to stop me cold.

"Be careful," she whispers.

The words detonate inside me. Concern. For me. Not fear. Not anger. Concern.

It shouldn't mean this much. I've been stabbed, shot, burned. I've had men pray for my death, beg for my mercy, curse my name. But never this—never a woman's soft voice asking me to take care because she wants me to come back.

My chest tightens in a way I don't have a name for.

I lean down, brush my lips across her forehead, inhaling her. "Always."

Her eyes follow me as I go, a tether around my ribs.

"I'll be back before you count too many sunsets."

I can't resist one more glance at the woman who's captured my stony heart. She waves. The feelings in my heart reach my lips. I smile.

On the helipad, the rotor blades stir. My men file in, stone-faced, their silence the armor of soldiers who've seen too much. I nod to the pilot, climb aboard, leather groaning under my weight.

As the helicopter lifts, the island drops away—a jewel in a vast sea. I picture her standing on the balcony, kimono clutched tight, watching me disappear. It's harder every day to leave her. Harder still not to bury myself inside her and never leave at all.

Because *Madonna Santa Maria*, it's so fucking hard.

I want to fuck her into the mattress. Put her on her hands and knees, cushion her belly swollen with my baby, grip those hips, and take her from behind like the feral beast I am. Watch in the mirror as her full tits bounce and her gorgeous face twists with pleasure while she screams my name.

My cock thickens at the thought, stiffening against my trousers. I shift in the seat, jaw clenched. Every night holding her is torture. Feeling her warmth against me, her curves soft and yielding, her scent filling my lungs— she stirs a hunger I can barely leash.

I think back to that first night, taking her virginity.

How tight her pussy was around my cock, how she gasped, clawed, clung. It's burned into me. And it will never be enough.

But I've sworn a vow. I won't touch her until she comes to me in need. Until she begs for me. Until she knows she's mine because she chooses it, not because I forced it.

So every morning, I take care of it in the shower, pumping my cock until cum spills down the tile, grunting her name while she sleeps a few feet away.

This woman is going to be the end of me.

By the time we land in Catania, the heat is already climbing, the city alive with horns and shouts.

Black SUVs wait, engines purring. My men fan around me, invisible to the crowd but undeniable in their presence.

Marcello is already at Club Petali, lounging like a cat who knows he's the most dangerous predator in the room. Faustino stands by the bar, sipping espresso.

We gather in the private office, walls padded in velvet, air heavy with the seriousness of the business handled within these walls.

Marcello leans back, eyes glinting. "Glad you made it, fratello. Time to see what the Bratva are selling."

Faustino slides a black coffee my way. "Luca wants eyes on this. No commitments yet. You observe. Form your opinion. Report back."

Marcello grins. "And maybe get your hands dirty. Always fun."

I sip, listening.

"Luca has no interest in human trafficking," Faustino reminds us, voice calm, factual. "Once he replaced your father as Boss, he began divesting from those… less savory involvements. Aside from a few high-end men's clubs where the women work willingly—including this one—he sold the other establishments."

Marcello shrugs. "Doesn't mean others don't see profit."

"Our primary focus is arms," Faustino continues. "We provide the largest assortment in the world, top-quality. From pistols to missiles. Clients seek us out. Revenue increased even after Luca stripped away the flesh trade."

Marcello's grin sharpens. "But the Bratva are making inroads. These new auctions—they supply the girls. We provide the club. Profits split. In our favor, naturally."

"And you want us to witness one." My voice is flat.

Marcello's eyes gleam. "Exactly. If we let them run unchecked, they get bold. If we partner, they bow. Luca and Ludovico want an informed opinion. Flavio will weigh in. But this is an opportunity, fratello. An opportunity for us to prove we're as powerful, as feared, as they are."

I lean back, balancing the coffee cup on my knee, thinking of Paolina's soft hand on my arm this morning. "Then let's see what our enemies bring to the table."

Marcello smiles like a wolf. Faustino nods once, calm as always.

The deal may decide how the Family moves against

the Bratva. But in my chest, another truth beats louder: I'll raze the world before I let any of it touch Paolina or our daughter.

Faustino and Marcello continue planning our next move.

I listen. But my mind drifts to my universe—my woman and our daughter.

Because no matter what this Family chooses, no matter what profits line their books, she will never see this world. Not my wife. Not my child.

Madonna Santa Maria, the thought burns through me, raw and absolute.

No one *will ever sell my daughter on a stage. Never shove her into a brothel. Never make her into a commodity for men like the Bratva to paw at. She will be safe. Hidden. Protected by walls no man can breach.*

For years, I didn't care who bled, who broke. I enforced the Family's will because that was my role. A made-man with a gun in his hand and nothing to lose. But now—now I have something to lose. Someone.

Two someones.

Paolina softens me when she looks at me with those moss-green eyes, when her hand brushes my arm and tells me to be careful. But she also sharpens me, steels me, because I will kill the world before I let it harm her.

And our daughter... she's already changed me. I feel it every night when I cradle Paolina's belly while she sleeps. Every morning when I take care of the ache myself so I don't wake her. Every time I catch myself imagining a future I never believed I'd have.

Family isn't just the Lucchese name anymore. It's Paolina. It's the child within her. And nothing—no business, no brother, no Bratva—will touch them.

Faustino breaks the silence. "How is she?" His tone is neutral, but I hear the weight behind it.

Marcello smirks. "How's our runaway bride? And the little heir?"

My grip tightens on the glass. I sip before I answer, voice low, clipped. "Healthy. The baby kicks strong. The doctor says both are well."

Faustino nods once. "Good. It's been quiet. No word from her father. None from Aldo."

My jaw clenches. "It stays that way."

Marcello chuckles, leaning forward. "So, she's softening you, *fratello*. Who would've thought Donatello Romano could be domesticated?"

My eyes cut to his, sharp enough to kill. "Don't mistake softness for weakness. She is mine. And I'll paint the streets red before I let anyone take her from me."

Marcello's grin widens, satisfied. Faustino only lifts his glass, toasting silently, as if he already knew I'd say it.

I drink, the whiskey burning down my throat, but nothing burns hotter than the vow carved into my bones: Paolina and our daughter will never bleed for this Family.

They're mine to protect. Mine to worship. Mine to keep safe.

At all costs.

CHAPTER 9

aolina

THE PHONE SHOULDN'T EVEN BE HERE. Donatello confiscated mine the moment he pulled me off that airplane months ago. I haven't had a number, a signal, a tether to the outside since. But somehow one slipped past him—Nora, the nurse, left a backup mobile in the nightstand after checking my blood pressure. Probably meant for emergencies. Probably thought I'd never notice.

I noticed.

It buzzes now, screen glowing an unfamiliar number. Curiosity wins over caution.

"Hello?" My voice is tentative, caught between fear and longing.

"Troia."

The word slams into me like a slap. Aldo.

My breath locks.

"You think you humiliated me? You think you can run from me and spread your legs for that bastard Romano? *Sporca puttana.* You're carrying his brat, and you think anyone will respect you? You're filth. I know where you are. You're not safe from me. I'll cut that baby out of you. Better yet, I'll fuck it out of you. Show you what a real man is like. Hell. Maybe I'll let you crawl back to me when he's done with you."

He laughs maniacally.

"Oh, and if it's his money you're after, I've got my own. The dumb fuck doesn't even realize I've been skimming from the shipments, moving guns on the side. He thinks he knows everything. *Stronzo.* He'd better watch his back."

His voice, so familiar once, is poison now. Rage slithers with every syllable.

I can't answer. Tears blur my vision. My hand presses to my belly, instinctively shielding. The baby shifts as if stirred by my panic.

"Dirty slut," Aldo snarls, louder now. "I'll tell your father what you are. He'll spit on you. He'll thank me when I put you back in your place. See you soon, troia."

The line goes dead.

I sit frozen, phone limp in my hand, body trembling with aftershocks of fear. My breath comes ragged, chest aching.

The door bursts open. I jump to my feet expecting Aldo. Instead, a guard enters, machine gun raised, sharp eyes search the room. "Signorina? I heard raised voices."

I can't answer. My throat burns as tears stream down my flushed cheeks.

He takes one look at my face and doesn't wait—he pulls out his radio. "Get D. Now."

I sit frozen, phone limp in my hand. My body trembles so violently I can feel the mattress shift beneath me. Donatello is going to kill him. He'll take Aldo apart piece by piece until nothing remains but blood and silence. And what then? Aldo may be a snake, but he's still famiglia. Killing him without sanction could ripple straight up to Luca and the Lucchese brothers. Even Marcello may not be able to stop his fate at their hands. I know enough to understand what it means when men like Donatello act outside the chain of command.

If he does this because of me… I'll be the problem. The ruin. The cause of a war in the family.

Thirty minutes later, the door bursts open. Donatello fills the frame, eyes narrowing when he sees my face. He crosses to me in two strides, crouches so we're eye level, his stare black fire. "What happened?"

"Nothing," I blurt out, clutching the phone tighter. "I just… I overreacted."

His gaze slices through me. "Don't lie." His hand clamps around my wrist, not painful, but unyielding. "Tell me. Now."

"It's nothing—"

"*No.*" His voice sharpens, steel over stone. "You never lie to me, Paolina. Ever. Or else."

Fear and shame tangle. "I don't want to cause trouble for you," I whisper. "For the family. If you hurt him—"

He scoffs, jaw flexing, a harsh sound that shudders through me. "One last time, *bella mia.* Tell me. Or I find out my way, and then your silence will matter less than the truth."

Tears sting my eyes. My throat closes. He waits, silent and immovable, until my breath breaks on the confession. "It was Aldo. He called. He… He called me names. Said I was a dirty slut. Said he'd take the baby. That my father would spit on me for what I've done." My voice shakes, falling to a whisper. "He said he'd find me. Fuck my baby from me. He's been stealing from the Family."

Donatello stills to stone. His grip tightens once, then releases as he stands. His expression is no longer man, no longer human. It's predatory.

"Good girl," he says, soft and terrifying as he rises. "Now I know exactly what to do."

I try to speak. Instead, I fold, sobbing.

He gathers me into his arms before the sounds finish leaving my mouth. "Shhh," he murmurs, tucking me under his chin. His palm spreads over my belly, protective, calming. "I've got you. He'll never touch you. Never touch her. Not while I breathe."

The tremors take a long time to ebb. My tears dampen his shirt. His thumb strokes slow circles on my back until exhaustion drags me under. My last awareness is of his lips brushing my hair.

"You're safe, *bella mia.* Sleep. I'll handle this."

DONATELLO

HER SOBS ECHO in my head long after she falls asleep. They crack something in me no bullet ever has. Aldo's voice came through this room like filth through clean water. I won't let it happen again.

I press a kiss to her temple, careful not to wake her, and ease from the bed.

Nora hovers outside the door. One look at my face makes her blanch.

"This your phone?"

She nods, stumbling backwards.

My hand lashes out and grips her arm like a vise, dragging her into the hallway, closing the double doors behind me. She cowers as my face lowers inches to hers.

"Are you a fucking mole, Nora?"

She trembles.

I shake her like a leaf trapped in the eye of a tornado. "Answer me, damn you."

"He—He forced me. Threatened to r—rape and kill my baby brother—"

"I don't give a fuck about your baby brother or you.

I'll kill you and your entire fucking family," I thunder as I shove her towards the soldiers. "Lock the bitch up in the dungeon. I'll deal with her after I kill that son of a bitch Aldo."

Her pleas for mercy trail behind me as I charge down the hallway.

"One of you stays with Paolina," I order. "No one enters. Not even God himself."

Downstairs, I dial Marcello. He answers on the first ring.

"Brother."

"Aldo called Paolina," I say. Voice flat. Controlled. The words vibrate with something darker beneath. "He threatened her. Threatened our daughter. And the fucker admitted he's been stealing guns, selling them off. That's why he shot Gino. It wasn't a mistake—he was about to rat Aldo out."

Silence. Then a hiss. "Where?"

"I'll find him. Tonight."

"Do it," Marcello replies. "End him. Don't worry about any blowback. I got you, brother."

Faustino joins the call. His tone is colder. "Make it slow. He's disgraced us long enough."

I end the call, already moving. My soldiers know by my stride not to ask questions. The helicopter waits, blades cutting the night. Sicily awaits, her blood in my veins and vengeance in my bones.

The warehouse reeks of oil and damp concrete. Chains clink as Aldo dangles from them, stripped to his shirt, arrogance gone from his eyes. My men delivered him like garbage. Naked and already bruised from their fists. My turn.

"Donatello—wait—"

I don't. My fist cracks his jaw. Blood sprays. His cry is high and ugly.

"You threatened *her*." My voice is low, deadly. "You threatened *my baby*."

"I—she—"

My knife is already in my hand. I press the blade against his mouth, then inside, prying. "You like to run it so much. Let's see how you do without it."

His eyes go wide. The muffled plea dies as I slice. His tongue severs with a gush of blood and piss. I stuff the slab of meat up his ass since he talks shit and wants to fuck with what's mine.

"Talk now," I snarl.

He gags, chokes, thrashes. My men snicker.

"See you in hell, motherfucker."

Eyes locked on his, I end him with one sure cut across his throat. His body jerks, sprays, stills. The silence that follows is cleaner than confession.

"Burn him," I order. "Scatter the ashes in the sea. Let the fish choke on him."

Hours later, I step into the villa, the weight of blood washed from me but still clinging in my chest.

The scent of jasmine greets me, soft, incongruous. Upstairs, our suite is dim, the sea murmuring outside. I nod at the soldier as he opens the doors for me.

I strip. Paolina stirs as I slide beneath the covers. Her eyes flutter half-open, searching. I draw her into me, pressing her back to my chest, one hand cradling the curve of her belly.

"Shhh," I murmur against her hair. "It's done. You're safe."

She sighs, already falling under again, and I hold her tighter, the echo of vengeance still humming in my veins, anchored only by the woman and child who are mine.

Forever.

CHAPTER 10

 *aolina*

THE SEA IS a restless thing tonight. It throws itself against the cliffs below the villa, then drags back with a sound like teeth gnashing in the dark. I sit on the terrace, the cashmere shawl Donatello bought for me wrapped tight around my shoulders and try to breathe past the unease coiled in my chest.

It's been two days since he left. He didn't tell me why. He never tells me where he goes when he boards that helicopter at midnight with his jaw set and eyes hard. But I know.

Aldo.

A month later and the memory of his call still crawls

across my skin, his words echoing: *dirty slut, I'll cut that baby from you.* Even now, bile rises at the sound of his voice in my head. And Donatello—he heard my confession, kissed the top of my head, and tucked me into bed like I was something fragile. Then he left, carrying fury like a blade in his hand.

It still gnaws at me—how Aldo knew. How he found me here when Donatello took every precaution, when this island is supposed to be untouchable.

Then it clicks. Nora.

Sweet, kind Nora, with her gentle hands and her careful way of checking my blood pressure every morning, her soft humming when she lays the stethoscope against my belly. She never meant harm. But kindness doesn't erase carelessness. I can picture it too clearly: a night off the island, wine flowing too freely, her guard slipping as she boasted to a friend about the employer who paid her in diamonds and discretion. *A runaway Corsetti bride, seven months pregnant, hidden away on a private island.* All it takes is one friend with loose lips of her own, and Aldo has his thread to pull.

I should hate her for it. I can't. She's human, weak the way we all are.

Donatello didn't kill her. He could have. Men have died for smaller mistakes. But when I asked where she went after Aldo's call, his answer clipped, final. "She's gone. Fired. No woman dies by my hand unless it's an extreme situation."

That's their code. Brutal. Absolute.

I can still see Nora's face in my memory, flushed from drink, laughing too loudly as words she couldn't take back slipped into the world. Her mistake nearly cost me everything. Yet Donatello only cast her out, sparing her when he would have already scattered a man in her place as dust at sea.

I don't know whether to be grateful or afraid.

I press both palms to my belly. The baby shifts beneath my skin, strong now, rolling like waves. Eight months. One left until my body is no longer just mine.

"You'll be safe," I whisper to the little one. "Your father promised. And when he promises..." My throat closes. "He keeps it."

The helicopter returns just before dawn. I hear it first —the deep *whump-whump* of the blades cutting the sky— before I see the lights through the curtains. My pulse jumps. I run a hand through my hair, heart hammering with something that feels too much like relief.

The front doors open, heavy, deliberate. Boots strike marble. I don't realize I've gone to meet him until I'm halfway down the stairs, silk trailing behind me.

Donatello looks carved from stone and shadow, shirt open at the throat, forearms bare except for tattoos. His eyes find mine at once. I stop, breath caught in my chest.

He crosses the foyer without a word, sweeping me into his arms. The scent of soap clings to him, but beneath it—faint, metallic—something darker lingers. I don't ask. I don't need to.

"You're back," I breathe against his collar.

"Always," he says, voice low, rough. His palm spreads over my belly, grounding us both. "I told you. You're safe. He'll never touch you again."

A shiver runs through me. My heart knows what my mind fears to name. Aldo is gone. Donatello made sure of it.

He takes my hand and strides towards the stairs.

In the suite, he strips off his suit without hesitation. The jacket slides from his broad shoulders and lands neatly over a chair. He works at the buttons of his shirt, revealing olive skin stretched over thick muscle, his chest a wall of strength carved by years of discipline, not vanity. The play of lamplight catches the hard ridges of his abs, the tattoos on his arms shifting with every movement.

Heat coils low in me as he steps out of his pants, leaving him in a pair of fitted briefs for a moment before pulling on black joggers and a long-sleeve tee. Even dressed down, he looks lethal, impossibly male. He isn't the man you see in glossy magazines, pampered and coiffed. He is power forged in the streets, in blood, in sweat—and God help me, my body responds to every inch.

He glances over his shoulder as he pushes up the sleeves to reveal his muscular forearms, voice calm. "Tell me about your day."

The question startles me. Not a command, not a demand. Just him… wanting to know.

"I had yoga," I manage, forcing my eyes up from the way his shirt stretches across his back. "Swam a little. Read outside."

"Not too much?" His tone sharpens slightly, protective. "The doctor said your blood pressure was climbing. You're not to overdo it."

I swallow, warmth flickering in my chest at his attention. Aldo never noticed me. My father never listened. But Donatello—he sees everything.

"It wasn't too much." I respond. "I promise."

"*Bene.*" He pulls the joggers low on his hips, then strides closer, eyes locked on me. "I want you rested. Fed. Strong. You and our daughter both."

I swallow against the lump in my throat. No one has ever spoken about me like that—like my wellbeing matters. Like I matter.

"Donatello…" My voice wavers. "Thank you. For caring."

Something shifts in his eyes, softer, deeper. He brushes a knuckle over my cheekbone, slow, tender. "Of course I care, *bella mia.* You're mine."

God help me. This man is going to break down my defenses.

"Now, how shall we spend our day?"

A chunk crumbles.

"A cruise," Donatello says, answering himself when I can't find words. "The yacht is ready. Come."

The gleaming vessel waits at the private dock, all

white lines and chrome against the sapphire-blue sea. A staff of three bows as we board, quiet and efficient. I should remember that I'm not free, that this is gilded captivity—but the salty air and sunlight stroking my skin make it hard to think of anything except how alive I feel.

We set out, engines humming, the coastline shrinking behind us until there's nothing but water in every direction. Donatello gives me a tour and then stops in the main cabin.

"Swim?" he suggests. "Bikinis are in your closet here."

I follow him, not sure I want to wear a bikini. Even without my big belly, I would never dare wear a skimpy swimsuit. Donatello lifts a handful of barely there pieces from a drawer. I linger in the doorway.

He cocks his head at my hesitation.

"*Bella mia*, your body is a lush playground. Never feel any way but sexy around me. I adore every one of your curves." His gaze skims my body, pausing at my full breasts. His throat works. "My favorite—your tempting tits."

I gasp. He chuckles.

"Change and we swim."

On deck, the Sicilian sun paints every one of his muscles in a golden sheen. My mouth goes dry. He glances at me, a smirk tugging at his lips, as if he knows exactly what I'm thinking.

I nod, trying to keep my face composed even as heat slides low in my belly. He helps me down the stern ladder and then dives cleanly, cutting through the water like a predator. His head pops up, and he raises his arms for me.

The Med is cool, shocking against my overheated skin. I laugh—really laugh—as I float on my back with the sun warming my face. Donatello surfaces near me, slick hair pushed back, eyes dark with hunger and something softer.

"Careful," he says. "Don't drift too far."

"I can swim," I protest, kicking away just to tease.

His hand shoots out, circling my wrist. *Bella mia,* you're carrying my world. You don't leave my sight."

My chest flutters in ways I don't want to name.

When we climb back aboard, towels and chilled lemonade are waiting. I sink onto a sunbed, the plush cushion cradling me, while Donatello drops beside me with casual grace. The baby shifts under my palm, rolling, and I whisper nonsense to her. Out of the corner of my eye, I see him watching, reverent, silent.

Lunch comes—fresh grilled fish, olives glistening with oil, tomatoes so sweet they taste like candy. We eat under the canopy. The sea spread endlessly around us.

"You're quiet," Donatello observes, spearing a piece of fruit with his fork.

"I'm… enjoying myself," I admit, startled by the truth.

His mouth curves, slow and satisfied. "Good."

Later, I stretch out on the sunbed again, silk cover-up brushing my skin. Donatello lies beside me, one arm folded under his head, the other reaching across the small distance to rest warm against my thigh. We speak little—just fragments. He asks about the book I was reading. I ask about his brothers carefully, curiously. He gives me pieces, not the whole.

It feels… normal. Too normal.

The sea rocks the yacht gently. The air smells of salt and citrus from the drinks the steward brings. My eyes grow heavy.

God help me, I think as I drift. *I'm happy. I shouldn't be, but I am.*

When I wake, Donatello is still beside me, watching the horizon as if he could command it to bow. His hand hasn't left my thigh. He turns his head slowly, catching my gaze.

"See? A good day."

I nod, throat tight, unable to answer. Because he's right. And every good day with him is another crack in my resolve.

Later, in bed, he pulls me against him as always. But tonight, I don't fall straight to sleep. My body hums with restless wanting. His arm drapes heavy over my belly, anchoring me. And lower, I feel him—hard, insistent, restrained. He never moves beyond holding me. But the restraint tonight feels like its own kind of torment.

My thighs clench. My breath stutters. I whisper before I can stop myself: "Donatello…"

He goes still.

I turn in his arms, meeting obsidian eyes that catch the moonlight. The heat in them sears me.

"You want me," he says gruffly. Not a question. A certainty.

"Yes," I whisper, my voice breaking. "Please."

He cups my face, thumb stroking my cheek. "I swore I'd wait until you were ready. Tell me you are."

I nod. Tears sting, but they're born of wanting, not fear. "I'm ready."

The groan that leaves him is guttural, torn from a place deeper than control. His mouth claims mine, fierce and reverent all at once. Gone is the ruthless enforcer who took my virginity with fire and force.

Tonight, he kisses me like a man starved, like a man given bread at last.

His hands map me slowly, reverently, as if he's memorizing each curve. The swell of my breasts heavy with milk, the roundness of my belly, the softness of thighs that ache for him. He whispers *bellissima, mia regina, la mia vita* between kisses, words that brand more deeply than his touch.

He sits up. Surprised, my eyes open to find him murmuring into his mobile. He ends the call and rises from the bed, hand extended towards me.

"*Bella mia*, come."

I don't hesitate.

Donatello takes my hand, not forcing, not commanding—just holding. We take our time as he leads me to the upper deck. The night air is warm, fragrant with sea air. Lanterns flicker along the railing, soft pools of golden light swaying in the breeze. Beyond them, the sea murmurs, endless and steady, as if it knows the rhythm of us before we do. A crew member created a low bed made with silk pillows and draped in a canopy of gauze that stirs like ghostly veils in the salt-sweet wind.

I stop short, breath catching. It looks like something from a dream. Too beautiful for someone like me to belong in. Too tender for the man I thought could only ever take.

But tonight, his eyes aren't a hunter's eyes. They're warm obsidian, reflecting lantern light, fixed on me as if I'm the only thing in the world worth seeing.

"Lie down, *bella mia*," he murmurs as he guides me.

I obey, sinking into the silks, the fabric cool and decadent against my overheated skin. He lowers himself beside me, bracing on one arm so his weight doesn't press me into the cushions. His other hand slides across the swell of my belly, reverent, protective.

"You're carrying our daughter," he whispers, lips brushing my temple. "And I swear I will worship you both."

It isn't possession. It's a promise.

His mouth trails down my cheek, over the corner of my lips, slow and savoring. I arch into him, the wanting too sharp to hold back. My fingers find the drawstring of his silk pajamas, fumbling them open until I can feel warm skin beneath my palms. He groans against my lips as he finally claims them fully. The kiss is unhurried but devastating. He tastes of red wine and salt air. He tastes of everything I shouldn't crave but do.

He undresses me carefully, reverently, as though my nightgown reveals a secret only to him. His gaze never leaves mine, even as he bares me. "Bellissima," he murmurs, voice husky with awe. "My queen."

I tremble beneath the weight of his words, of his hands.

When his mouth closes over my breast, his tongue teasing until I cry out, he groans softly. Not from conquest. From reverence. As if every sound I make is a prayer answered.

"Donatello…" My voice is a plea, a confession. "I need you… please."

He eases me back into the nest of pillows, hovering above me. His hand cups my cheek again, thumb stroking the dampness beneath my eye. "Tonight, I don't take, Paolina. Tonight, I give."

When he finally enters me, it's slow, deep, filling me inch by inch until I can't tell where I end and he begins. My breath stutters. My body yields. It doesn't feel like surrender—it feels like finding something I didn't know I was missing.

He moves with exquisite patience, hips rolling in a rhythm that makes my toes curl and my heart ache. His forehead rests against mine, eyes locked, as if he's carving the moment into eternity.

"I love the way you look at me," he whispers, voice breaking. "Like I'm more than what I've done."

I choke back a sob, pulling him closer. "Because you are."

The words unspool between us like gossamer, fragile and indestructible all at once.

Pleasure builds inside me, not violent or over-whelming this time, but steady, like a tide pulling me higher. When I crest, it's not a shattering. It's unraveling. My body arches, clinging to him, breaking and remaking itself in his arms.

He follows, groaning my name like a prayer, spilling into me as his lips claim mine again.

Afterward, he doesn't roll away. He stays wrapped around me, kissing my face, my hair, my swollen belly. His hand strokes the curve, protective and adoring. "You've given me everything," he murmurs. "And I'll spend my life giving it back."

I press my forehead to his, tears slipping free. "Donatello…"

He kisses them away, each one, until there's nothing left but the sound of the sea and the whisper of the gauze above us, cocooning us in a world that feels like it could belong only to us.

My fingers trace his jaw, rough with stubble. For the first time, I don't think of running.

I think of staying.

I think of love.

And it terrifies me almost as much as it thrills.

As dawn brushes the horizon pink, I watch him sleep, this man who was supposed to be my captor and has become something I can't name. I press a kiss to his temple and whisper so softly it might be only for me.

"I don't want to fight this anymore."

The baby shifts beneath my palm, as if agreeing.

For the first time, I imagine a future not built on escape, but on us.

CHAPTER 11

aolina

THE WAVES ARE STILL ROCKING in my body when I wake the next morning. My dreams carry the scent of salt and citrus, the taste of grilled fish, the feel of Donatello's palm heavy and protective against my thigh as we lay side by side on the yacht.

Now back in the villa, the memory is too sweet. Too dangerous.

Am I sure this is what I want? Or were my hormones talking for me?

I rise slowly, hand bracing against the small of my back. My belly has become its own horizon, a perfect curve stretching taut beneath the silk of my nightgown.

Eight and a half months. The baby is restless, twisting and rolling as if she can't wait to make her debut.

I pad to the balcony and push open the doors. The sea sprawls below, endless, blue as glass. Morning sunlight warms my face. For a moment, I let myself breathe in the beauty, pretend it's mine by choice.

"Too early to be standing so long."

His voice startles me. Donatello leans in the doorway, already dressed in black joggers and a fitted long-sleeve tee. Damp hair clings to his temples from his shower. He looks freshly carved, freshly dangerous.

"I'm fine," I murmur, though my back aches, my ankles swollen from yesterday's indulgence on the yacht.

He crosses the room, his shadow falling over me, then his hand—broad, warm—spreads across my belly. The baby kicks beneath his palm. His expression shifts, softening into something I almost can't look at.

"She's strong," he says quietly. "Like her mother."

Heat pricks my eyes. I look away, pretending to study the sea. "Don't flatter me. I've done nothing but lie around like a spoiled queen."

"You're carrying my child," he counters, tone sharp but reverent. "There is no greater strength."

The words hit me harder than they should. Aldo would have called me lazy. My father would have scolded me for weakness. Donatello praises me. It disarms me in ways bullets never could.

Later that morning, the nurse fusses over me with her blood pressure cuff, the doctor notes the baby's heartbeat, and the chef sends up papaya with honey and toast cut in perfect triangles. My life here runs on a rhythm orchestrated by Donatello—structured, controlled, safe.

After the appointments, I wander the courtyard, maxi dress brushing my ankles. Alberto's assistant waters the bougainvillea, the air fragrant with blossoms. A guard trails discreetly behind, far enough to give the illusion of freedom.

My thoughts try to sway me. *If not for the kidnapping... if not for the violence that brought me here... this could be paradise.*

I press a hand to my belly, whispering to my daughter, "What will we do, *piccola*? Will we stay in this golden cage? Or will we run when the chance comes?"

By noon, Donatello finds me in the library curled in a velvet chair. He fills the doorway like a shadow, arms crossed, expression unreadable.

"Come," he says. "Eat with me."

I follow him down to the terrace, where lunch waits —grilled chicken, fresh salad, fruit chilled on ice.

He pulls out my chair, an old-world courtesy that unsettles me as much as it charms me.

We eat together, silence threaded with the clink of silverware. His gaze flicks to my plate, checking that I eat enough. I bristle, but the attention warms part of me.

When I push my fork aside, full, he asks, "Tired?"

"A little."

His jaw softens. "Rest after. The heat is stronger now. I don't want you fainting."

I snort softly. "You sound like the doctor."

"I sound like a man who won't see his woman collapse in front of him." His eyes pin mine, dark and steady. "Do not mistake care for control, *bella mia*. They are different."

I look away, because if I don't, I'll fall deeper into something I no longer want to escape.

The afternoon drifts in quiet—reading, napping, the baby kicking strong against my ribs. When I wake near dusk, Donatello is sitting at the desk, gun parts spread neatly before him, hands moving with precise care. For a moment, I just watch. The way he balances brutality with gentleness when he turns to check if I'm awake.

"You should have woken me," I murmur, stretching.

"You needed sleep." His eyes soften.

He cleans his weapon, reassembles it, and tucks it back into its case. Then he comes to me, bending, lips brushing my temple. "Dinner soon."

I nod.

After dinner, we sit on the balcony again, the sea black velvet under the stars. The gauzy curtains stir around us, the night scented with jasmine.

"I thought of leaving today," I admit softly.

His gaze sharpens. "Leaving?"

I swallow. "If this wasn't… what it is. If I wasn't your captive. This place could be perfect."

His jaw tightens. "Not captive. Protected. Mine."

The words hang between us. I want to argue, but I

can't deny the truth of part of it. He has kept me safe. He has kept our daughter safe. And he's proven I'm his.

And maybe—God help me—I like it.

When he gathers me against him, muscular arms circling my belly, I don't resist. I let myself sink into his warmth, my head on his chest, and wonder if we could stay this way forever.

DONATELLO

SHE FINALLY SAID it without saying the words.

I need you.

Not with her mouth, but with the way she reached for me on the deck bed—silk pillows, gauze breathing in the breeze, the sea keeping time while I made love to her like a prayer I'd been afraid to speak. Not taking. Giving. Her hands in my hair, her eyes on mine, the trust a man like me doesn't earn but bleeds for.

I replay it in the quiet—how she softened under my palms, how she opened for me with a sigh that sounded like surrender and salvation in the same breath. Every groan lodged in my throat still lives there. I could close my eyes and map the moment by touch alone—the curve of her belly under my hand, our daughter rolling like she wanted to witness her parents choosing each other at last.

And then tonight on the balcony—*I thought of leaving today.* The sentence slid from her mouth like a blade wrapped in silk. She kept her gaze steady, waiting for me to rage. I didn't. Rage is simple; what I felt wasn't. It was colder, cleaner. A vow hardening into bone.

Let her think it. Weigh it against the taste of freedom she used to dream about. Trace her old maps in her head and tell herself there's a world where she walks away. But there isn't. Not anymore.

I won't let her go.

I've let other things go. Territory. Profit. Men who mistook courage for suicide. Not Paolina. The woman who moans my name with her hands shaking on my shoulders and sleeps with my palm splayed over the baby we made. The woman who whispered *thank you for caring* like it was the first time anyone ever did. She belongs here—in my bed, in my house, in my life— because I built the one place on earth nothing can touch her. Protection is a cage only if the door locks from one side. I'm building us a door that opens inward, a door she *chooses.*

So, I keep doing it. Every day, every hour. Patience when my body riots. Restraint when the animal howls. I feed her when she forgets to eat. Make sure the doctor catches a problem before it becomes a threat. Stand between her and the world, and I don't blink. Take her on the water so she can breathe where the horizon is wider than memory. Listen—really listen—when she talks about little things no one ever cared to notice.

Which fruit the baby makes her crave. Which pages in a book make her smile.

I do the quiet work that never made my name feared but will make it loved.

She's changing me. People like to say a man can't soften without being made weak. They've never tried to keep something sacred alive. It takes more strength to hold tenderness steady than it ever did to put a gun in a man's mouth. I still have the gun. Still remember how to use it—just remember why now.

When she told me she'd thought of leaving, I watched her throat move, the tiny tremor she didn't know I saw. I could have argued. I could have said, *not captive, but protected* and left it sharp as a command. Instead, I tucked her in, changed out of the suit that still smelled faintly of ash and ocean, and asked about her day. *Tell me about your day.* She looked at me as if I'd done something extraordinary. I hadn't. Men have been asking their women that question since the world found language. But the men she knew didn't. I will. Every night. Until the answer includes, *I love you* without her even realizing she's said it.

Because it's there already. In the way she watched me lift in the sun, in the way she waved at the helipad. It's there in how she falls asleep in the courtyard and lets me carry her all the way to bed, heavy and precious, trusting me not to drop what is mine.

A few more weeks. Maybe less. Our daughter will arrive, and the world will tip again. I've seen men turn stupid with fear in delivery rooms—men who run rackets that could swallow cities go to their knees in front of a woman's pain. I'm already on mine in ways I swore I'd never be. Yet I'll rip the sky down before I let either of them bleed more than nature requires. I've arranged the doctor, the nurse, the backup, the generator, a second chopper fueled and waiting. I've drawn a circle around this island like a blade.

Anyone who crosses it dies.

But this isn't about the plan. It's about the promise.

Bella mia, you thought of leaving. You can think about it until thinking bores you. While you think, I'll be here making the leaving feel less like freedom and more like loss. I'll give you breakfasts in the courtyard and quiet hands at midnight; I'll give you safety you can taste and a future that doesn't ask you to shrink to fit it. I'll keep my monsters outside the gate and my warmth inside these walls until the choice stops feeling like surrender and starts feeling like home.

I can hear her breathing from the chair, slow and even, the peace I never had in me until she put it there. The wind off the balcony whispers. The sea answers. My hand itches to go to her belly again, to say good night to the little life we made with promises and heat.

A couple more weeks before our baby is born. Time enough.

She already needs me. I feel it. She already loves me. I see it when she forgets to guard her eyes.

But I want the words.

I want *I love you, Donatello,* spoken into my mouth, against my throat, into the skin over my heart where I'll keep it. I want the vow to travel the same road my name does when she moans it, to live where breath meets truth.

So, I wait, work, watch, worship.

And when she's ready, I'll take what's been mine since the first time she looked at me across a crowded room and didn't look away.

Not her body. Not her obedience.

Her yes.

Because I already said it, if only in my mind and actions.

I love you, Paolina.

CHAPTER 12

 *aolina*

THE PAIN STARTS like a tightening deep in my back, low and sharp, pulling me out of restless sleep before dawn. At first, I think it's just another false alarm—I've had Braxton Hicks for weeks now. But when the second one rolls through ten minutes later, my breath catches. By the third, I can't stay still.

I shift in bed, my hand reaching instinctively for Donatello. He's there, as always, curled against me, his palm curved protectively around my swollen belly.

"Donatello," I whisper. My voice cracks. "It's time."

His eyes open instantly, with no haze of sleep. Obsidian sharp, deadly alert, as if his body's been waiting for this moment. *"Cristo."* He's already moving, swinging out of bed, grabbing his phone and barking orders in rapid-fire Italian.

Within minutes, the villa comes alive—guards in motion, the nurse and doctor rushing in. Faustino and Marcello appear from the rooms they've been staying in while they hold vigil with Donatello, calm but intense, like two dark pillars in the hall. My breath hitches again as another contraction claws its way through me.

Donatello is at my side in a blink, sliding an arm around me. "Breathe with me, *bella mia*. In. Out. I've got you."

His calmness steadies me, but fear gnaws at my chest. The island feels suddenly too small, too far from the rest of the world. "I can't do this here," I gasp. "I need a hospital."

"You'll have one." He sweeps me into his arms as if I weigh nothing, carrying me down the stairs.

The double doors burst open to reveal the helicopter already whirring on the pad, blades cutting the dawn.

The flight is a blur of pain and motion. I'm stretched across Donatello's lap, his hand gripping mine, his other hand stroking my hair. Faustino sits across, jaw tight, eyes steady on me as if willing me strength. Marcello murmurs into his phone, already clearing landing space at the hospital.

"You're strong," Donatello whispers, lips against my temple. "Stronger than anyone. Our daughter is strong too. We're almost there."

The contractions come faster, stealing my breath, my

pride, my composure. I cling to him, burying my face in his chest, letting the steady thrum of the rotors drown out my fear.

The hospital is chaotic. Bright lights, sharp scents, voices barking orders. And then—faces I never expected.

My mother. Tears streak her cheeks, her hands reaching but not touching, as if afraid I'll vanish. Behind her, my father stands grim, pale with fury and something else I can't name.

"Paolina," Mamma breathes, voice breaking.

I can't answer before another contraction grips me, dragging a scream from my throat. Donatello's arms tighten around me, his glare slicing through the crowd. "Back. All of you. She doesn't need your bullshit."

And then I see them—his parents. His mother, regal in black silk, eyes sharp and assessing but with a glimmer of warmth. His father, older, stoic, with the same brutal jaw as his sons. They nod once, as if acknowledging me as theirs.

I'm rushed onto a bed, wheeled through double doors, nurses swarming. Donatello never lets go of my hand. Faustino and Marcello follow close, emanating power at the threshold. Our parents remain outside, the weight of their worlds pressing against the glass. Guards block the hallway and stand at my door.

Inside, the pain rips me apart. Sweat blinds me. My screams echo off tile. Even so, he's there—Donatello, bending close, voice low and fierce: "Breathe, *amore.*

Push when they tell you. I'm here. I won't leave. Not ever."

Hours blur. Pain, pushing, tears. Then—the cry. Piercing. Strong.

Our baby girl.

They place her on my chest—tiny, warm, perfect. My body shakes with sobs I can't control.

Donatello bends, his forehead against mine, his voice raw. "*Nostra figlia.* Our daughter." His hand trembles as it cups her head. "*Ti amo, bella mia.*"

The world tilts. Donatello Romano loves me.

"*Ti amo, amore mio,*" I murmur thickly.

"*Grazie a Dio.*"

The smile he gives me shines brighter than Times Square on New Year's Eve.

For the first time, I don't think about running. There's no doubt in my mind. We're staying.

The decision settles over me like a cloak I didn't realize I'd been wearing all along. No running. No escape plan humming at the edges of my thoughts. Just here— this man, this child, this family that is ours whether I wanted it.

The room smells of antiseptic and lavender. My body feels emptied, wrecked, yet filled at the same time with something fierce and new.

Cosima. Our daughter.

The nurses lift her gently from my chest to clean her, weigh her, check every detail.

Donatello never leaves her side. He watches with a

predator's focus, as if daring anyone to falter. When they swaddle her, his enormous hands are the first to cradle her.

I blink through tears as he stands over her, his dark head bowed close. The enforcer everyone fears… holding a newborn like she's made of spun glass.

"Cosima," he whispers. "Order. Beauty." His voice cracks on the word beauty, a sound I never thought I'd hear from him.

I want to reach for them both, but I can't move, not yet. My body is too heavy, too raw. A nurse helps me into a fresh silk nightgown, the pale fabric cool against my overheated skin.

Another gently brushes my hair, pulling it back from my damp face. I should feel like porcelain being arranged, but for once I don't mind. I want to look… assured. Confident of our family. Our love.

When I'm settled against pillows, Donatello lifts Cosima and crosses to me. He places her in my arms once more, then turns to the doorway. "Bring them in."

The door opens, and the families file inside.

My mother gasps softly, tears shining. My father follows, jaw clenched, his silence louder than any curse. Donatello's parents enter, his father grim but approving, his mother smiling faintly at our baby. Faustino and Marcello stand beside their brother.

I'm surprised when Boss Lucca Lucchese enters, flanked by his twin and Underboss Ludovico and their adopted brother, Consigliere Flavio. Their presence is its own seal of approval, and my heart swells with quiet joy.

Donatello stands tall at the bedside, one hand on my shoulder, the other resting lightly on our daughter's blanket. His voice carries deep and certain.

"Her name is Cosima Romano. *Cosima*—for order, for beauty. She carries both in her blood. She is ours."

The words are both announcement and decree.

For a breath, the room is silent. Then congratulations ripple through: Donatello's mother kisses my cheeks, murmuring blessings; Faustino grips my shoulder, steady and warm; Marcello smirks but his eyes soften. My mother touches my hand, whispering, *"Bellissima, tesoro.* She's perfect."

My father lingers back, eyes hard. Anger coils within him. I can see it, but he says nothing. Not here. Not now. He knows better than to challenge Donatello at this moment, when all power radiates from him like heat. Not to mention the imposing presence of the head of the Family.

Inside, my emotions swirl. Pride. Relief. Love that hurts. Fear of what it means to belong so wholly to this man and this Family now.

I look down at Cosima, tiny lips parted in sleep and know one thing for certain: I would walk through fire to keep her safe. And Donatello—God help him—so would he.

When I lift my gaze to him, he's already watching me,

eyes molten, unreadable. His hand tightens just slightly on my shoulder. Possession. Protection. Love.

And in that moment, with everyone gathered, I feel the shift—the old life closing, the new one sealing around me like a favorite blanket.

Surprise hits me again when Donatello quiets everyone, takes my hand, and drops to one knee. He raises a black velvet box. The top pops open to reveal a stunning diamond ring. My eyes widen.

He clears his throat.

"Paolina." His voice is low but strong, carrying to every corner of the room. "I took you. I claimed you before you understood what it meant. But I have no regrets—not for one moment—because it brought me here. To this. To you. To *her*." His gaze flicks to our daughter, then returns to me, molten with intensity. "You and Cosima are my life. My future. My everything. And I want the world to know you are mine—not just by my word, not just by our child, but by choice. By vow. By love."

The diamond catches the light, scattering rainbows across the walls. My chest tightens until I can barely breathe.

My father shifts, stiff and silent, but no protest escapes him. He knows better than to interrupt. My mother clasps her hands, eyes shining. Faustino and Marcello exchange a glance, both amused and approving. Donatello's parents watch with quiet pride. Lucca gives a slow, solemn nod.

Inside, my thoughts spin. *Kidnapped. Possessed. Protected. Desired. And now... this. Marriage. Permanence. A lifetime bound to a man who tempts me and softens me in ways I never thought possible.*

Donatello's thumb strokes across the back of my hand, grounding me. "Say yes, *bella mia*. Make me whole."

My heart pounds. My throat is dry. Everyone is waiting. But all I can see is him—this lethal man kneeling in front of me with a diamond and a promise, his eyes stripped of every mask but love.

A sob catches in my chest. "Yes," I whisper, tears spilling. "Yes, *amore mio*."

The room exhales. Applause, murmurs, congratulations ripple around us, but Donatello doesn't hear them. He slides the ring onto my finger, rises, and captures my mouth in a kiss that silences everything else.

When he pulls back, his lips brush mine with a vow only I can hear: "Forever, Paolina. You'll never run again."

At last, I don't want to.

Donatello

THE DIAMOND SETTLES on her finger as if forged there. Her whisper of *yes* still vibrates in my chest, louder than any oath I've ever sworn to my brothers.

The room erupts in polite applause, murmured blessings, forced smiles. I don't give a damn. None of them matter. Not Marcello with his smirk, not Faustino with his quiet nod, not my father's measured approval or her father's thin-lipped fury. Nor Lucca, Ludo, and Flavio's confirmation. The only thing that matters is the woman in front of me—my woman—wearing my ring, holding my child, finally saying yes.

I kiss her, slow and claiming, ignoring the crowd. When I pull back, her lips are swollen, her eyes glassy, her breath caught. *Mine.*

Triumph rolls through me, sharp and hot. They all saw it. Every one of them. The Corsetti girl, the runaway bride, the woman they thought would shame us—she is here, bearing my name with my heir, agreeing to be mine in front of every witness that counts. No man will ever question it again.

But deeper than the triumph is something I don't let anyone see. Relief. Gratitude. The way my chest eases hearing her speak the words I've waited for.

Still, possession threads through it. I lean close, my mouth brushing her ear so only she hears. "Forever, Paolina. You'll never run again."

She trembles, but she doesn't pull away.

I turn back to the room, my arm circling her shoulders. "She's mine," I announce, voice carrying like a decree. "My fiancée. My family."

And as I look down at her with Cosima swaddled at

her breast, I vow again: I'll destroy the world before I let either of them bleed.

Forever starts now.

CHAPTER 13

3 Months Later
Paolina

A YEAR AGO, I was standing in tulle I didn't want, veil heavy on my head, about to walk toward a man who betrayed me with my so-called best friend. A year ago, I was nothing but a pawn in my father's game, a Corsetti daughter handed off to Aldo Buratti like I was property.

Now, I stand in silk I chose, in a villa overlooking the Mediterranean, our daughter Cosima cooing in my mother's arms, and I realize the truth: that failed wedding was the beginning of my life.

The wedding planner transformed the courtyard for our ceremony. Arches draped with bougainvillea, lanterns glowing as the sun sinks, tables lined with crystal and white roses. Cosima gurgles softly when Marcello tickles her chin. Faustino watches her like a sentinel. My mother dabs her eyes. My father stands stiff, silent, but present—because even he knows there's no undoing what Donatello and I are now, especially in the presence of Lucca, Ludo, and Flavio.

Donatello—*my* Donatello—waits for me at the altar in a perfectly cut black tuxedo, his dark hair slicked back, his eyes locked on me as if nothing else exists.

I walk toward him, bouquet trembling in my hands. Each step is steady, certain. My heart swells with a joy so fierce it almost hurts.

When I reach him, he takes my hand, bringing it to his lips. His thumb strokes over my knuckles, right where the diamond he gave me still sparkles.

"*Bella mia,*" he whispers. "You came with me one year ago. Today, you stay."

Tears prick my eyelashes, but I smile. "I thank God every day Aldo was stupid enough to bang Cara." My voice cracks with laughter and wonder. "If he hadn't, I wouldn't have the husband of my dreams. Or our daughter."

Our vows are simple, spoken in front of both families, but I don't hear anyone else. Just him. Just the certainty in his voice when he says *forever.*

When he kisses me, the courtyard erupts in applause, but all I feel is his mouth on mine, the strength of his hands at my waist, the heat of a love I never thought I'd find.

A year ago, someone broke me. Tonight, I'm whole—wife, mother, queen in the only kingdom that matters.

And as the stars rise over the sea, I hold my husband's hand, glance at our daughter, and know with absolute certainty. This is the life meant for me to live.

DONATELLO

THE MUSIC hums low under the clink of glasses and the murmur of guests. I step away from the courtyard for a moment, Cosima tucked safe with her *Nonna*, Paolina glowing in her gown as she laughs with the women. My brothers gather near the fountain, the air thick with cigars and whiskey.

Marcello spots me first, his grin wicked. He lifts his glass high. "To Donatello—taken off the market. Who would've thought someone could tame the beast?"

Faustino smirks, quiet but sharp. "Not tamed. Redirected."

Lucca leans back, the Boss's presence filling the circle without effort. "A Romano who finally puts family before business." He raises an eyebrow. "It suits you, fratello."

Ludo snorts, always the cynic. "It suits him because she's beautiful and gives him heirs. Let's not pretend this is all sentiment."

Flavio chuckles, smooth as ever. "Even sentiment has

its place, Ludo. You'd know that if you weren't such a stone."

Marcello claps my shoulder, laughing. "Still—marriage? You? I thought you'd die before you put a ring on a woman's finger."

I meet his grin with a slow one of my own. "Careful, Marcello. Your time will come."

He throws his head back, laughing louder. "Mine? *No, no.* I'm built for pleasure, not chains. Let the rest of you rot if you want matrimony. I'll keep my freedom, thank you."

Faustino raises his glass, voice low. "Freedom has a way of ending when you least expect it."

Marcello rolls his eyes, but the color high in his cheeks betrays him. "Not me. Never me."

I sip my whiskey, watching him with the calm of a man who knows better. "We'll see."

The circle breaks into laughter, the sound echoing across the courtyard. But I file Marcello's protest away. Because I've learned one thing above all—love hunts when you least expect it. And when it does, even beasts like us fall.

I wave them off and spin on my heel. Their laughter follows me. But my eyes fix on the most important people in my life.

Paolina. My wife. My queen. The mother of my child.

She holds Cosima against her hip, our baby's dark curls already thick, cheeks flushed pink from too much attention. Paolina's silk gown shimmers in the glow, her smile soft as she coos down at our daughter.

I've slit throats for less beauty than this. I've killed men for daring to touch what wasn't theirs. Tonight, I stand here knowing I'd burn down kingdoms to keep them.

A year ago, she was running from me. A year ago, I swore I'd make her mine. I thought I was the hunter, thought I was the one who stalked, claimed, possessed. And I was.

But she conquered me too.

Every night she let me hold her belly, each morning she let me feed her, all the times she laughed when she thought she shouldn't—she broke me down without ever trying.

Now she looks up, catches me staring, and my chest tightens in that way I've learned not to fight. She lifts Cosima slightly, as if presenting her to me. My blood, heir, proof that fate bowed to my will.

I cross over to them, laying a hand on Paolina's waist, bending to kiss our daughter's tiny head. Then I press my lips to my wife's temple, murmuring so only she hears: "Forever, *bella mia*. You and her. Always."

She leans into me, sighing like she believes it. And that's all I'll ever need.

The world can fear me. Men can whisper my name with dread. But at the end of it all, here under Sicilian stars, the truth is simple—

I took her. She kept me.

And I'll never let her go.

~

THANK you for reading *Taken by the Enforcer*! If you enjoyed the book, I would so appreciate your review as they make a huge difference for indie authors.

Don't want it to be over? Need more?
Join my newsletter for an exclusive bonus epilogue with
a new pup for this foursome!
https://BookHip.com/PHDQLJR

WANT to read more about the Taken Series? Turn the page for a preview of *Taken by the Capo: A Dark Mafia Romance*.

BE sure to join my Facebook Group for a community who love my spicy worlds facebook.com/groups/charmainelouisebookscoterie!

For early access to my current works and bonus books, visit my Ream Stories reamstories.com/charmainelouisebooks.

PREVIEW TAKEN BY THE CAPO: A DARK MAFIA ROMANCE

*F*ive *Years Ago*
　　　Messina, Sicily
Marcello — 21

"OH, I won't take your pussy cherry. But I will pop that ass of yours, *bella*. Your future husband will never know his fiancée isn't a virgin."

Giada Lombardi shivers as my warm breath skitters over the shell of her ear. Lips trail open-mouthed kisses down her neck to the juncture of her shoulder, where my teeth nip the sensitive flesh. A moan slips from her parted lips as she shudders against the wall pinned between my forearms.

I smirk at her reaction.

Niccolò Lombardi would have my balls if he knew my intentions for his seventeen-year-old eldest daughter, already promised to another man. The highest-ranking capo of my family's organization—*La Cosa Nostra*—Lombardi runs his slice of the pie and crew of soldiers with an iron fist.

But he's no match for mine—Marcello *The Hammer* Lucchese, third-born son of Vincenzo the Boss.

I live by our family's motto, *Want It. Take it.* And by my Taran Tactical Glocks.

A made man since my first kill to mark my thirteenth birthday. Nothing comes between me and what I want. Even as a child, I took whatever the fuck I wanted from others. If they refused, I hammered them. First with the toy car I wanted, then with my fists. They gave willingly or crying.

And Giada Lombardi will give crying my name as I pound my cock in her virgin ass.

My erection punches against the zipper of my bespoke tuxedo trousers. I grind my well-endowed junk against her pussy as my fingers tighten around her throat and one hip. My dick throbs as she gasps for air. Her pink, manicured fingernails claw at mine.

I lick up her throat to her slack mouth. The tip of my tongue rims her glossy lips. She moans while heavy lids lower over bright blue eyes. My tongue dives in. It sweeps the wet warmth to tangle with her tongue as she gives willingly.

Good girl.

Better to give me what I want than for me to take it.

Not that I need to take from women. Oh, no. They

drop to their knees or spread their legs for the baby face killer. The contrast of my soulful mink brown eyes and clean-shaven face with my reputation as a ruthless assassin makes their pussies wetter than the Ionian Sea off the coast of Sicily. I could drown a blissful death as I eat their pussies. Whores, socialites, mafia princesses all succumb to my mystique.

And Giada falls the hardest.

Her knees wobble as I kiss her breathless. Soft mewls escape her mouth. Hips gyrate as she meets the grinding of my pelvis. Yeah, she's ready.

I spin her around to face the wall. I can't help but to grind my cock against her round ass, driving her hip bones against the silk wallpaper. A good foot shorter than my six feet, four inches, I bend my knees to align her ass with my groin. Braced by my muscular thighs, I thrust up, lifting her to the balls of her feet in the high heels.

My hands place her palms against the wall as I press my front to her back. She moans and pushes her ass against me. Warm breath comes out in pants while her eyes squeeze shut. I can hear the thoughts as they race through her mind.

So good.

My father will kill me!

Oh, God, Marcello!

I snicker and nip at her nape. She squeaks.

"Keep your hands on the wall," I order as I press mine

on top of them. "Do not move unless I tell you. Understand, *bella*?"

She nods. Then yelps and her eyes pop open as my palm connects with her ass through the evening gown. She cranes her neck to look at me. I bunch her dress around her waist and pull her hips back.

"Wha—"

"Words, *bella*. I will have your words."

Her eyes flutter closed as I pepper her ass exposed by a skimpy thong with a flurry of spanks. The corners of my mouth quirk up and nostrils flare as I watch her creamy skin bloom a rosy pink.

"Use. Your. Words."

I punctuate each word with a spank that jiggles her reddened butt cheeks.

"I—I—I understand!" She wails, face flushed like her ass.

"Good girl."

I slide the tip of my middle finger along the inside of her thong, down to her pussy lips. The silk comes away soaked.

Giada likes it rough. Naughty girl.

She gasps and struggles to close her legs when my finger rims her slick pussy lips and slips inside to the second knuckle.

"No!"

"No?" I ask as my finger slides in and out of her tight pussy, eased by her natural lubricant.

"Y—You said you wouldn't touch me there. You said my butt, Marcello."

My wicked chuckle makes her tremble. Then she moans as I increase the pace of the thrusts.

"I never said I wouldn't touch your pussy, *bella*. And I am a man of my word."

Her pussy walls quiver around my thick finger. My ring finger flicks her engorged clit, and she goes off like a rocket.

Pussy grips my finger. Juices gush into my palm. Mouth forms a perfect O as a throaty moan pours from between her parted lips. My thighs press against the backs of hers to keep her from collapsing to the floor as her entire body convulses.

Damn. Has no man set her off?

What a dumb fuck her fiancé must be.

My fingers continue their magic, drawing out her orgasm until she's still. A satisfied smirk spreads across my face as I lean into her ear and nip the delicate lobe.

"You're ready to take my cock in your ass now, *bella*—"

I jerk away and rise to my full height as the sounds of shouts and screams infiltrate the room. My gaze swivels to the door of the meeting room next to the grand ballroom in the hotel owned by my family. The clicking of high heels on marble and the heavier thudding of men's shoes as guests run past the door adds to the unexpected chaos.

What the fuck could happen at my older sister Gemma's engagement party to Giada's brother Renzo?

I don't waste time figuring it out. Instead, I grab Giada by the arm and pull her to the conference table. Dragging a chair away, I push her forward.

"Hide under the table until your family comes for you. Do not leave this room. Understand?"

This time, I don't demand her words. She nods as her wide eyes flick between me and the door where the hysteria increases. Without hesitation, she scampers under the table. I roll the chair back in place before I rush for the door. I slam the lights off and crack the door open.

Automatically, my hands go to my Taran Tactical Glocks in the holsters beneath my tuxedo jacket and click the safeties off. I whip them out as I step from the room. The door closes behind me with a soft snick. Guests race past me, fleeing the ballroom. I run to it.

"Fuck you, Ludovico! Fuck you too, Luca! And to hell with you, Flavio! You think you're tough shit as the Boss' sons? It's time for the Lucchese rule to end! It may not be me. But someone will take you out! End your fucking line for good!"

Renzo glares through blackened eyes as he kneels before my older brothers. Bloody spittle lands on Ludovico's shiny patent leather dress shoes. His face remains impassive as he holds one of his Heckler & Kochs to Renzo's forehead.

Around them—also on their knees—Niccolò, his two

younger sons, and his top soldiers glare with eyes full of hatred. Luca, Flavio, and some of our soldiers train their guns on them.

In search of my parents and sisters, Gemma and Allegra, my gaze roves over those remaining in the ballroom. The Lombardi women—except from Giada—huddle in a corner surrounded by more of our soldiers. Other capos and their soldiers stand to the side. But no sign of the rest of my family. My heart lurches in my chest as I run to my brothers' sides.

I aim my guns at Niccolò. He spits at my feet. I don't flinch. But my fingers itch on the twin triggers.

"It won't be you."

The crack of the gun as it discharges a bullet into Renzo's skull reverberates around the ballroom. His head snaps back at the force as a hole appears between his eyes. Another crack signals the shot to his heart. Women scream.

I don't have to look at Ludovico to know the process. Our father taught us to shoot between the eyes and in the heart to ensure the kill.

Renzo Lombardi is no more.

His father roars at the death of his heir and rises to one foot.

I shoot his kneecap.

He screams in agony and falls to his side, covering the blown joint with his hands. Blood oozes past his trousers and between his fingers.

"Do not kill him, Marcello."

Luca's calm command stills my trigger fingers.

"End the others."

Without hesitation, Flavio, our soldiers, and I kill them. The room erupts in gunfire, screams, and shouts. A single gunshot aimed at the ceiling silences the ballroom. All eyes shift to Luca.

The eldest of the Lucchese siblings at twenty-five and the identical twin to Ludovico stalks towards Niccolò. My brother moves with the grace of a predator as he focuses his sharp brown eyes on the fallen capo. Their eyes meet. Neither cowers.

"You dare to kill our father while our mother rides in the car with him on their way to your son's engagement party to our sister? You break the code of no harm to women and to children. So you can take over what my family has run for generations? The Lucchese's rule *La Cosa Nostra*."

My heart skips a beat.

However, years of trainings—including beatings by my father's hands—prevent me from displaying any reaction and damn sure no emotion. I sense the eyes of the other capos and their soldiers on my brothers and me. I remain still with my guns at the ready.

"You dare to speak to me like I'm someone beneath you, boy?! You're still shooting blanks. I don't give a fuck who you think you are."

Ludovico and Flavio flank Luca. Niccolò gives them a scathing look and spits at their feet.

"Marcello, bring Giada from wherever you were fucking her."

The son of another capo utters a string of Italian curses. But he shuts his mouth with a quickness when a soldier faces him.

"You filthy animal! If you laid a fucking hand on my daughter—"

Ludovico knocks the words from Niccolò's mouth with the butt of his gun. A glob of blood mixed with broken teeth lands on the floor. Wordlessly, Ludo steps back.

I stride from the ballroom and return with a frightened Giada gripped by the elbow.

"Father!"

She jerks. But I hold her fast and drag her to Luca.

"My father taught us an eye for an eye—"

"No! Please! Please, Luca! I beg you! Do not kill my daughter! We know nothing!"

The Lombardi matriarch's cries ring out in the ballroom. She pleads while we stare impassively.

She cries, and my mother is dead.

I give zero fucks. Kill the bitch.

Interestingly, Giada's fiancé remains silent. I flick my gaze from him back to Niccolò. He rises to his knees. A grimace crosses his face at the pressure on the shattered joint. He clasps his hands together and lowers his gaze in supplication.

"Luca, Giada's mother is correct. They know nothing

of my plan to overtake your father. The women are innocent—"

"As was my mother."

Niccolò flinches at the deadly tone. But he continues to beg.

"Please, Luca, let them live. You killed my sons and my soldiers involved. Kill me now. But have mercy on Giada. Please."

Silence descends.

Giada and the other women cry softly.

Two gunshots ring out.

The body crumples to the ground.

Screams and shouts fill the air.

***

Click the Link Below or Visit http://bit.ly/ CharmaineLouiseSheltonBooksList For Your Copy

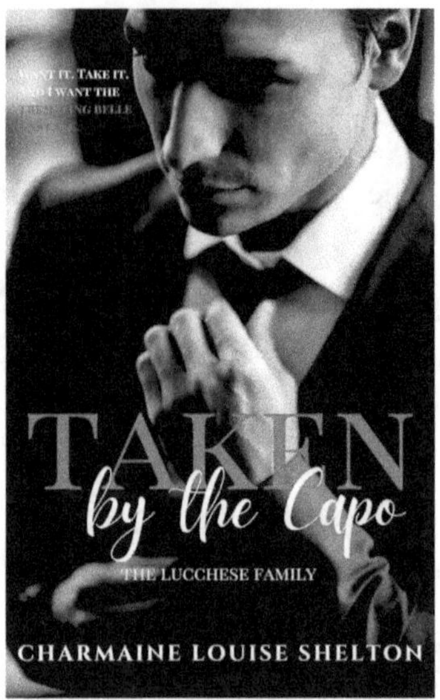

Taken by the Capo

ALSO BY CHARMAINE LOUISE SHELTON

STEELE INTERNATIONAL, INC.

A BILLIONAIRES ROMANCE SERIES

Discover My Desires Sebastian & Lola Prequel

(Available Exclusively to Subscribers)

Fulfill My Desires Sebastian & Lola Part I

Heighten My Desires Sebastian & Lola Part II

Gift My Desires Sebastian & Lola First Christmas

Ignite My Desires Roger & Leonie Part I

Stoke My Desires Roger & Leonie Part II

Justify My Desires Roger & Leonie Part III

Deepen My Desires Sebastian & Lola Part III

Capture My Desires Malcolm & Starr Part I

Embrace My Desires Malcolm & Starr Part II

Cherish My Desires Malcolm & Starr Part III

A Trilogy of Desires Sebastian & Lola Parts I-III

STEELE INTERNATIONAL, INC. - JACKSON CORPORATION

A BILLIONAIRES ROMANCE SERIES CROSSOVER

THE MEN OF STEELE WORLD

Spark My Desires Milly's Men

Incite My Desires Carter & Genevieve

Awaken My Desires Alan & Tabitha

TAKEN SERIES: LUCCHESE FAMILY

Taken by the Enforcer: A Dark Mafia Surprise Baby Romance

Taken by the Capo: A Dark Mafia Revenge Romance

BILLIONAIRE WOLVES SERIES

WOLF SHIFTER FATED MATES PARANORMAL ROMANCE

MIAMI

Jagger The Awakening

(Available Exclusively to Subscribers)

Jagger The Temptation

Rust The Rejected

Tag The Redemption

Viggo The Obsession

Dylan The Rogue

Billionaire Wolves of Miami — The Complete Collection

NEW YORK

Signy's Mates

Signy Claimed

Signy Forever

Series Playlist

Complete List bit.ly/CharmaineLouiseSheltonBooksList

CharmaineLouiseBooks.com

To read her current works in progress, visit her Ream
Stories reamstories.com/charmainelouisebooks.

ABOUT CHARMAINE LOUISE SHELTON

Charmaine Louise Shelton loves a dominant Alpha hero —human, shifter, or vampire—as long as he's a billionaire and sexy as sin! Her romance novels take readers into the heroes' glitzy, glamorous, steamy worlds as they chase after independent women who unexpectedly capture their hearts.

Want to experience some more? Follow her on social media on your favorite channels below. Read her current works in progress at her Ream Stories bit.ly/Charmaine LouiseBooksCoterie. Join her newsletter for the latest updates, releases, and more bit.ly/CLBooksJoin Newsletter.

Find her at:
CharmaineLouiseBooks.com

Fulfill Your Desires.

DEDICATION

To my awesome and dedicated beta readers and ARC Team, my amazing author friends, and this incredible community for their support.

And most of all to you, my loyal readers who love these couples as much as I do.

Thank you!

Fulfill Your Desires.

xoxo
Charmaine Louise Shelton